WESTWARD, MY LOVE

Elaine L. Schulte

BOOKS

of the Zondervan Publishing House
Grand Rapids, Michigan

A Note From the Author:
I love to hear from my readers! You may correspond with me by writing:

>   Elaine L. Schulte
>   1415 Lake Drive, S.E.
>   Grand Rapids, MI 49506

ACKNOWLEDGMENTS

With special appreciation to the staffs of the Nevada Historical Society, State Historical Society of Missouri, and Rancho Santa Fe Library, as well as to Alice Ball, Jackie Barrett, Marie Butler, Caroline Helms, Virginia Henderson, and Alice McIntire.

With a heart full of love for Richard,
editor extraordinaire.

CHAPTER 1

ABBY WINDSOR TALBOT lifted her sapphire-blue evening dress decorously as she descended the grand staircase of Miss Sheffield's School for Young Ladies. *Be careful,* she reminded herself. The numerous petticoats under her bouffant bell skirt caused the steps, hewn of local New York marble, to be treacherous, and it was precisely here that one was most apt to be caught for lack of grace and propriety. Since supper, she had harbored a vague premonition that something would go amiss—and this was no time for complications. Her Class of 1845 graduation was only weeks hence.

"Wait for me, Abby!" her roommate, Rose Wilmington, whispered insistently from the upper hallway.

No one else was about, and Abby lingered on the staircase landing, enjoying the early evening sunshine streaming through the open French windows. The soft air held a scent of lilacs and distant pines, and birds twittered across the estate garden, with its splendid statues.

Rose was breathless as she arrived on the landing.

"Abby—do you know that you look like a painting for the Louvre? Yes, you do! *Blonde Beauty on a Marble Staircase!*"

"Oh, Rose! I only look nice because you dressed my chignon and I'm not wearing a wretched uniform."

After wearing the gray school garb day after day, month after month, she had scarcely recognized herself in the mirror: silk evening dress and sapphire pendant as blue as her eyes, golden hair wound into a French chignon, long white gloves. She would be seventeen years old tomorrow, and finally she was beginning to give every appearance of her new maturity.

She glanced at her roommate and best friend, who wore a pale green silk gown that set off her raven black hair and brown eyes. "You're a vision yourself!"

"It *is* being free of those uniforms," Rose agreed, and they both laughed with the delight of it.

Starting down the last flight of stairs, Abby took pleasure in the luxurious entrance hall with its exquisite Persian rug and a magnificent portrait of the school's founder. She was hardly conscious of a maid's opening the ornately carved double doors, but at the sight of two men visitors at the door, Abby paused for an instant. The men were well dressed in black broadcloth suits and vests, and white linen shirts with high stocks around their necks. "*Two Gentlemen Calling*," she whispered to Rose, continuing their divertissement of bestowing titles upon people and scenes as if they were paintings.

"Perfect!" Rose suppressed a smile as they proceeded to the marble entrance where the men now stood.

Abby glanced at them again. They looked familiar. Had she seen them before? The younger man, perhaps thirty, was tall and bearded, darkly handsome with intense blue eyes. The gray-haired gentleman was clean-shaven and rather avuncular; for a moment she had the impression that he might step toward her, but he apparently reconsidered.

Passing by them, Abby and Rose entered the adjacent ballroom with its frescoed ceiling, potted palms, and graceful French Empire furniture. The entire west wall of French doors was open to capture spring breezes.

"Who are the men?" Rose inquired as they hurried to join their classmates to practice the mid-May reception and musicale that would take place on Saturday.

"I don't know."

Rose blinked in surprise. "I thought perhaps you did. The younger one is so handsome . . . and romantic with that dark beard. And those blue eyes! Like the sea at Marblehead!"

"Oh, really, Rose!" She turned to see the maid escort the men out of their line of vision. "I suppose they only appeared familiar at first."

Abby forgot the visitors at the sight of her classmates in their bright flounced and ruffled gowns instead of the usual gray uniforms. "If only I had my sketching pad and watercolors, I could capture this scene forever."

Abby noted Rose's perfume. "*Fleur-de-lis?*"

Rose smiled impishly. "*Fleur-de-lis.*"

"What if Miss Sheffield notices?" Their headmistress was adamant about *her* young ladies not using artifices such as face colors and scents, which she termed "nothing but common."

"I don't care," Rose returned with daring. "William gave it to me, and I feel closer to him when I wear it."

"You *are* hopeless!"

"And you're too sensible. Wait until you fall in love!" Rose beamed. "Just three more days until William arrives!"

Abby gave a laugh. "I may be sensible, but I'm afraid that you're far beyond curing!"

"I hope that someday you'll be smitten too," Rose replied with her usual good humor.

Abby shrugged. Would she wear Cornelius Adams's perfume herself if perchance he presented some to her? It was difficult to imagine. On the other hand, Rose, like many of her classmates, was eighteen and engaged to be married this summer. The only romance between Cornelius and herself, she sometimes thought, was at their families' insistence.

"Ladies, please!" Miss Page clapped her hands again, and her charges quieted, only to be interrupted by Miss Sheffield's assistant hurrying into the ballroom. The two women spoke quietly, their eyes darting momentarily to Abby, then the advisor said, "Miss Talbot, you may be excused to go to Miss Sheffield's drawing room."

Why would Miss Sheffield want to see me? Abby wondered as she left. *Does it concern the two men?*

At the headmistress's drawing room door, she nervously smoothed her skirt, tidied her chignon, and knocked. After a moment Miss Sheffield opened the door, her expression as severe as her dyed black hair skinned back into a perfect bun. "Won't you please come in, Miss Talbot?" she invited, her chin held high, accentuating her long neck.

The green drawing room, with its gracious European furniture, was an inappropriate accompaniment to Miss Sheffield's severity, Abby decided as she stepped in. The two men she had seen at the front door rose from their chairs, and Abby suddenly recognized the older. "Why, you're . . . you're my Uncle Benjamin from Missouri!"

He smiled warmly, his brown eyes twinkling at her words. "I'm pleased that you remember, Abigail," he said, stepping forward to take her hand in his. "It's been ten years since I called at your home in New York City."

10

"I thought you looked familiar when I saw you at the door, but you wore a beard!"

"And had no gray hair," he added with a chuckle. "And you weren't yet such a beautiful young woman. I was almost certain I recognized you . . . and your Grandmother Talbot's sapphire pendant, which suits you so perfectly."

Abby's hand went to the pendant at the modestly scooped neckline of her blue gown. "Thank you." Noticing the laughter lines around his eyes and mouth, she guessed that her uncle was a convivial person, perhaps even jolly at times, although now his expression grew serious again.

He turned to the young man beside him. "Perhaps you also remember Mr. Daniel Wainwright."

She extended her hand to him, having been aware of his intense blue eyes resting upon her. "Yes . . . I believe I do. Now I know—you visited my family together. You were a student . . . at Harvard, I think, Mr. Wainwright."

Daniel Wainwright's hand engulfed hers. "Exactly. "I'm surprised that you remember. *I* was the beardless one then."

She smiled. "Yes, of course." Ordinarily she did not care for bearded men, but his wavy dark beard suited his manner and arresting face; she would love to attempt his portrait. And she did remember him! In fact, he had made such an impression upon her that she had indulged in fantasies about him for weeks after his departure.

"Won't you all be seated?" Miss Sheffield suggested. "I regret that there is unpleasant news for you, Miss Talbot."

"Unpleasant news?" Abby repeated as she settled uneasily on the rose-colored settee beside her uncle.

"And now, Mr. Talbot, if you would please proceed."

Her uncle cleared his throat. "I'm afraid that it

concerns your parents, Abigail. It seems that there was a boating accident in the Mediterranean, a most unfortunate accident—"

"Yes?" Abby felt a stab of fear. "Were they injured?"

He shook his head. "I'm afraid not. The fact is that . . . that they have both passed on. Fortunately they did not suffer, which is a blessing—"

"You mean they are d–dead?" Abby asked, stunned.

"Yes, child," her uncle replied with sympathy. "They have gone on to the next life."

Tears burst to her eyes. "But they are on their return voyage from France now! They are to be here for graduation!" Her mouth trembled and she caught her underlip with her teeth.

Miss Sheffield said stiffly, "Compose yourself, Miss Talbot. There is a great deal to be accomplished at times like this. You must not lose control of your emotions."

Despite the turmoil spinning in her head, Abby managed a tremulous, "Yes, ma'am."

"Abigail, my dear," her uncle began, "I know that this comes as a dreadful shock to you." He spoke on, but the words merely floated about her . . . something about her looking like her Grandmother Talbot, who was so wonderfully strong, something about clinging to that thought.

Miss Sheffield spoke up. "You have my deepest sympathies, Miss Talbot. I too had to summon up the courage to endure the death of my parents, and I assure you that you will."

Abby stared blindly at her. "They were to be here for my graduation—"

"Your graduation appears to be another problem, Abigail," her uncle said. "I am now your legal guardian, and I've had to make numerous decisions. Your Aunt Jessica and I are your only living relatives, and we invite you wholeheartedly to live with us in Missouri. We have a very pleasant house in Independence—not as grand as your parents' mansion on Union Square, of course."

"In Missouri!" Her parents had said that Uncle Benjamin lived on the frontier, in the wilderness, next to Indian Territory. "Thank you, but I don't know—"

"We don't expect your answer yet, child."

She had been born and reared in New York City before attending Miss Sheffield's School. The house on Union Square was her home; she had assumed she would live there until she married and perhaps even then for what she had expected to be a pleasant, unruffled life.

Her uncle's kindly voice spoke on, and Abby could only understand that she must leave with them tomorrow morning, that they would have a week to deal with affairs at her parents' house on Union Square . . . including a memorial service. She quailed at the prospect of a memorial service—a rite without even a last glimpse of Mother and Father—then leaving for Missouri. It was inconceivable!

"But I must graduate!" she protested. "It was so important to Mother and Father! No other school would do—"

Uncle Benjamin reassured her, "I'm certain that you will be given your diploma since there are only a few weeks until graduation. I understand that you are a very fine student—"

"I beg your pardon," Miss Sheffield said, "but we do not graduate young ladies who depart early. We have policies, and we are forced to uphold them, or this school would lose its reputation."

Uncle Benjamin's face turned florid. "Not receive her diploma when school is nearly finished? Under the circumstances, I find that unbelievable."

Miss Sheffield sat even more erectly in her chair. "Unfortunately, Miss Talbot's tuition for the

13

semester remains unpaid. I expected it would be settled upon her parents' return from Europe . . . before the graduation ceremony, of course.''

Uncle Benjamin inhaled deeply. "Then I am afraid, madam, that you would have been in for an unpleasant surprise.'' He looked regretfully at Abby. "I had hoped to break this all to you rather differently, child, but the fact is your father has lost more and more money over the past years. If he had lived, he might have been able to extricate himself from his financial difficulties since, after all, he was a vice-president of one of the largest banks in the country.''

"I don't understand . . ." Abby said, incredulous.

Her uncle replied sadly, "The estate is bankrupt.''

"Bankrupt? That's impossible!'' They'd always had money for anything they wanted. What could have happened? Father gambled, of course, and Mother called him improvident, but to be bankrupt—"Surely someone has made an error!''

"Unfortunately not,'' her uncle said. "I know that this must be shocking, and I will show you the books, but it is clear that you must move West with us . . . unless, of course, you have other prospects.''

Other prospects? He meant prospects for marriage! Did he know of her parents' hopes for her and Cornelius?

Benjamin Talbot interrupted Abby's thoughts. "You have two options, Miss Sheffield. Either I pay Abigail's tuition and you give her the diploma . . . or I pay nothing. I require your decision now.''

Indignant, Miss Sheffield said, "Very well. You will have the diploma tomorrow morning upon receipt of funds. I trust you will keep that as confidential as I intend to keep your affairs.'' She stood up in dismissal. "Please call for Miss Talbot promptly at ten o'clock. If there is nothing further, I shall see that her trunks are sent to her room now.''

Abby swallowed with difficulty. Her parents were

dead—*dead!*—and it seemed she was expected to act as if nothing upsetting had happened while her emotions flew about like a moth with hideously singed wings.

She found Daniel Wainwright watching her. "Courage," he said, his voice deep and vibrant. "Courage in trouble is half the battle."

"Yes," she replied shakily. "I'll try to remember." Oddly, she did not resent his advice. In the drawing room Daniel Wainwright had given off an aura of great inner strength. Her eyes caught in his blue gaze a moment too long before she bid the men a more tremulous good evening than she wished.

Upstairs, Abby blindly pulled her clothing from the chiffonier and armoire until everything was piled and folded atop her bed. Fortunately most of her paintings, sketch books, brushes, colors, pencils, and other art supplies were already stored in boxes.

She decided to set aside a favorite watercolor of the school garden as a parting gift for Rose, and, sorting through her work to find it, discovered an early attempt at a self-portrait. She had drawn herself with golden hair curling like a child's below her shoulders, great blue trusting eyes, an ordinary straight nose, sweet smiling lips, and a serene expression that had never known grief nor fear of the future. *Happiness* seemed an apt title. How differently she would depict herself now. Tonight her self-portrait would be of a young woman torn with anguish.

Finally her two trunks were delivered, and she stuffed her possessions into them, even her despised gray school uniforms—wool for winter and starched linen for spring and fall; after all, her father had purchased them, and if there was no more money she might be forced to wear them. As it was, she would have to wear one home. Her recently acquired womanly shape caused her russet traveling dress to be too tight. She was a late bloomer, like Mother . . .

At the thought of her mother, Abby's hard-won courage shattered into millions of sharp, brittle fragments. *Oh, Mother!* Hot tears rolled down her cheeks. And her father gone too! He had been such a handsome and dashing man—full of love for her, bursting with pride at her every accomplishment. "Your wish is my command, princess," he had said since her childhood. And he had given her everything she ever desired.

She was sobbing disconsolately when Rose returned to the room and asked in shock, "Abby—what is it? What's happened?"

"My parents—" Abby began, and between sobs, the heartbreaking words were finally spoken.

Rose caught her in her arms. "Oh, Abby . . . my poor, dear Abby . . . what will you do?"

Abby shook her head. "I don't know! I don't know! I don't want to live on the frontier with savages!"

At length she quieted and they sat on Rose's bed in bewilderment. "We must try to think clearly, to consider the options," Rose suggested. "Maybe Cornelius will propose immediately now and, under the circumstances, you could marry right away. You could stay with me in Georgetown, and we . . . we could have a double wedding! That would solve everything! It would be so lovely . . . not perfect now, of course."

Abby wiped away her tears and blew her nose. "I'm not sure that . . . Cornelius loves me. We've always only been . . . well, I suppose one would call us friends. Our families have thrown us together, but now that the money is gone—"

"Oh, bother!" Rose replied. "Any man in his right mind would be happy to have you just for yourself. Why, you've turned into one of the most beautiful girls in the class. Besides, Cornelius's family has enough money to last for centuries. What does it matter if you have none?"

Abby's spirits lifted only slightly.

"You'll see, Abby; it will all turn out fine. Place it in God's hands. Don't worry. You need a good sleep."

"I don't know," Abby repeated. She lacked her roommate's faith, although Grandfather Talbot had been an eminent clergyman in Boston years ago. Her father, the middle son, had been . . . well, she supposed that the word was *rebellious*. Lately her parents had turned to Emerson; his transcendentalism was the current rage, though her mother did take her to a nearby church on Christmas and Easter. As for Miss Sheffield's School for Young Ladies, it was progressive and had no chapel; a minister called twice a week to teach religion, but the class was not required, and Abby had taken advanced art courses instead.

Despite Rose's optimism, Abby endured the worst night's sleep of her life. Toward morning she lay quietly in the warmth of her covers, not wanting to disturb Rose, drifting between wakeful agony and troubled sleep, watching the sky turn from black to pale gray and then take on a pinkish glow. She had always been intrigued with changing light, but this morning she watched it with dread. At length she heard Rose's stirring.

"Abby?" Rose whispered from her bed, sounding less groggy than she did most mornings. "Are you awake?"

"Yes," Abby replied, gazing out the window.

"I-I hope you'll always be my friend."

"Oh, Rose!" After last night's bout of weeping, Abby thought she was all cried out, yet now hot tears rolled down her cheeks again. Even Rose had lost her optimism, and Abby gave another sob before quieting. "I want always to be your friend."

Rose leaned up on an elbow. "If you decide not to marry Cornelius . . . if—well, no matter what you decide to do, promise that you'll write."

17

Abby retrieved the handkerchief she had placed under her pillow last night. "I promise. I—I promise I'll write wherever I go." She turned to the window again.

After a long while her roommate asked, "What are you thinking about so quietly, Abby?"

"That I'll never wake up in this room again, that I'll never see another sunrise from this window . . ."

Rose said thoughtfully, "I imagine your life will change a lot, especially if you live on the frontier."

"Yes, I imagine it will," she responded sadly.

The wake-up bell sounded through the hallway, and Abby heard Rose climb out of bed.

"Aren't you getting up?" she asked.

"Not yet. They can't call for me until ten o'clock." Abby inhaled deeply. "When the girls ask about me, please tell them that I—that I can't bear saying goodbye."

"Miss Sheffield says that we must confront reality and carry on."

"I don't care. I'm going to try to sleep now." She pulled the covers over her head, trying to blot out everything. Much to her amazement, she slept and slept, right through the breakfast bell until nearly eight o'clock.

Upon rising, she placed the watercolor she had selected for Rose on her desk. Moments later, she discovered a note tucked in the frame of her mirror and a small package wrapped in white tissue standing nearby on her own desk. *I'm not going to wish you a happy seventeenth birthday*, Rose had written, *only that something wonderful will happen to you today, and that you have a happy year. God bless you, Your dear friend, Rose.*

HER SEVENTEENTH BIRTHDAY—she had forgotten all about it! With a catch in her throat, she folded the note and tucked it into her dress pocket, wondering what Rose might have given her. It was nearly impossible to shop out here in the countryside. Tearing the tissue away from the small package, she was overwhelmed. *Fleur-de-lis* . . . the treasured bottle of perfume that Rose had received from William! Abby steeled herself against more tears at the generous gesture made by her loving friend.

CHAPTER 2

AT NINE O'CLOCK THE PORTER ARRIVED for Abby's trunks, and after the ten o'clock class bell, one of the maids knocked at the door. "Yer wanted downstairs, Miss."

This morning she had only her gray starched linen uniform to lift decorously as she stepped down the marble staircase; the only attractive feature of the frock was the lacelike edging on its white, pointed collar. She wore her black school cloak and black cabriolet bonnet. Her appearance differed from schoolday outings only in that she had not braided her hair; golden curls spilled rebelliously from under her bonnet. She hoped that Miss Sheffield would witness her act of defiance, but there was no sign of the headmistress.

Uncle Benjamin and Daniel Wainwright stood near the door, smiling up at her encouragingly. As she joined them in the entry, her uncle produced an envelope. "Your diploma. You can always use it if you want to teach school. Your Aunt Jessica has hers, and she sets great store by it."

"Thank you very much," Abby replied gratefully. "I hope that someday I can repay you for your—your kindness."

"Nonsense," he replied as they started outdoors. "We are family, even if we don't know each other well yet."

Outside in the sunshine, she was heartened to see that old Joseph was driving the family carriage. He wore his handsome black livery and tipped his cap to her and said, "Mornin', Miss Abigail." Perhaps life would not be as dire as she feared after all, she thought before he solemnly added, "My sympathy, miss."

Her spirits sank at the reminder. "Thank you, Joseph."

"May I assist you?" Daniel Wainwright asked.

As he helped her into the carriage, she was far too aware of his nearness, of the strength of his hand under her elbow. Catching her breath, she inhaled the flowery scent of *Fleur-de-lis* that she had daubed behind her ears. Did Daniel Wainwright smell the perfume too? Embarrassed at her unseemly thoughts and behavior, she straightened the folds of her gray uniform as the men stepped into the carriage and settled on either side of her.

Old Joseph glanced at her soothingly as he closed the carriage doors, and they sat in silence while he climbed to the driver's seat. She heard him urge on the horses, no doubt flicking the reins lightly over them; then their hoofs clopped against the worn cobbles of the circular drive.

She was unable to resist turning back toward the stone mansion. Sunshine beamed through the towering elms and oaks that framed Miss Sheffield's School for Young Ladies, reflecting off its windows; near the entry, urns of daffodils lent brilliant color. Instead of feeling resentment at her inglorious departure, she took pleasure in the school's loveliness and was grateful to have painted it and the gardens so often. Now the paintings would provide vivid memories.

She could hear her father's voice saying again as he so often had, "We want you to have the best of everything." Her parents had been generous to her, even though they were often more aloof than she might have wished.

Turning to her, Uncle Benjamin said, "Our time is limited and it behooves us to discuss matters, Abigail."

"Please do."

He briefly described the situation: all of the bank stock had been liquidated over the past years and now the house on Union Square and its furnishings had been sold to pay the creditors. He continued, "I'm afraid that I've already had to dismiss most of the staff at the house. I did retain Joseph and Molly until the end of the month since we need Joseph and the carriage, of course. Molly is still the housekeeper, and she will also cook. I've had to make many decisions in a hurry, Abigail. I have done my best."

"I'm sure that you have. It—it couldn't have been easy for you to come across the country to New York so unexpectedly. I do appreciate all that you've done."

"Don't be too grateful until you see what we've accomplished, child. Daniel knows most of the bankers and merchants in the city. Without him, affairs would not have gone as smoothly as they have. Daniel is like a son to me. He lived with my family through most of his childhood, and I trust him implicitly. He will deal with matters after we leave."

"Thank you, Mr. Wainwright." She recalled now that he had been an orphan taken into her uncle's family.

"It's my pleasure to repay your uncle in a small way for his help when I needed it," Daniel responded sincerely. He hesitated, then added, "I would be more pleased if you called me Daniel."

Miss Sheffield would probably not approve, but Abby said, "Very well . . . if you like. While we are on the subject, the girls at school called me Abby. I much prefer it."

"Then Abby it is," her uncle said.

Daniel said, "Abby is beautiful, far more suitable."

"Thank you." She thought that if he were a flatterer, this was the first sign of it; he had, in fact, struck her as far too honest and intelligent for subterfuge.

The sun was setting when the carriage entered Union Square, where the splashing fountain in the park sparkled reddish-gold in the sunset. Neighborhood children rolled their hoops home under the trees, and ladies and gentlemen strolled along the gravel walks. As the horses turned into the circular driveway in front of the brown sandstone Talbot mansion, Abby noted the pink rhododendron in bloom. She looked at her beloved home sadly as Joseph brought the horses to a stop at the front steps. "Who purchased the house?" she asked as she stepped down from the carriage.

"Bankers from Philadelphia," Uncle Benjamin replied.

"It doesn't seem possible that it would be sold so soon," she remarked. And it didn't seem fair!

Daniel remarked, "Houses on Union Square are always in demand. It's an excellent location."

Abby felt powerless. "Yes, I daresay it is."

Molly opened the front door, dressed in her ample black dress, her round face framed by gray curls escaping the bun at the nape of her neck. "Welcome home, Miss Abigail," she said with her Irish lilt, tears clouding her eyes. "Oh, my dear . . . my little one!"

Abby flew into her arms. "Thank you, Molly. I'm grateful that you and Joseph are still here."

"We're pleased to help what we can. I'm only sad that things don't look like they should."

23

Abby glanced around at the white marble-floored entry. The Persian rug was missing, as were the French chandelier and the ancestral oil paintings that had lined the walls.

She walked about, heartsick at the barrenness. Everything was gone—furniture, china, crystal, silverware, even the harp and old harpsichord that had come from her mother's family in Boston. In the library she said, "I didn't expect it to be like this . . . that they would take even the books." None of the leather-bound volumes in the library remained, only copies of *Graham's Magazine, Godey's Ladies' Book*, inexpensive pamphlets, and the family Bible. It seemed a wonder that they left the Bible since it was like new, seldom having been used.

"*Barrenness*," she said, disconsolate.

Daniel said, "I beg your pardon?"

"It's only a—a game that my roommate and I played, entitling people and scenes as if they were paintings."

He too surveyed the rooms. "Yes, *Barrenness*."

Her uncle appeared distraught too. "I had the servants' table and chairs brought into the dining room for now, and their serving plates and dishes. I've tried to be practical. We do have to eat, and there are provisions in the house."

"And upstairs?" Abby asked dismally. "Is the furniture missing there too?"

"I retained some of the armoires and beds for now, and the furnishings for Molly and John above the carriage house."

"I'm so very tired," Abby admitted. "Would you mind if I go to bed? I'm sure there is still much to accomplish—"

"Nothing that we can't accomplish tomorrow," her uncle said. "The best thing for you is sleep, child."

"Yes." She reached up and kissed his cheek as she might have her father's. "Good night then, Uncle Benjamin."

Daniel waited with every appearance of embarrassment. Did he think that she might kiss him too? Well, he did not have to worry on that account. She reached out to shake his hand. "Thank you for standing by," she said. "Good night, Daniel."

She began to withdraw her hand, but he drew it to his lips and bestowed a light kiss on her fingertips.

"Good night, Abby," he returned with a curious glow in his blue eyes.

She turned in a flurry of astonishment. It was no longer fashionable for men to kiss ladies' fingertips in New York, but then Daniel had traveled widely; he was a man of the world. *Gallant Kissing a Young Lady's Hand,* she thought ruefully as she hurried away. It was simply a polite gesture.

As she ascended the stairs, she noticed the pale ovals, squares, and rectangles on the white walls marking spaces where family portraits had once hung. The portraits had ranged from the Windsors—her mother's side that had immigrated from England and claimed royal descendancy—to Charles Talbot on her father's side, Duke of Shrewsbury, who was Prime Minister of England in 1714. Her father had told her, "Your lineage goes back to the Talbot who fought with William the Conqueror at Hastings. You have illustrious relations on both sides. Do nothing to shame the family name, my dear."

How heartbroken her father would have been by all of this!

Upstairs in her room she tried to ignore the disappearance of most of the Venetian furniture she had loved. At least she had a bed. She undressed, hanging her gray linen uniform on a door peg. Noticing a bit of stiffness in the pocket, she slipped in her hand and discovered Rose's note.

Abby stood in her petticoats and read the words again. *I'm not going to wish you a happy birthday, only that something wonderful will happen to you*

*today, and that you have a happy year. God bless
you. Your loving friend, Rose.*

She had forgotten since this morning that it was her
seventeenth birthday—and what a miserable day it
had been. She had never been so unhappy in all her
life, which did not bode well for the remainder of the
year. As for something wonderful happening today,
there had been nothing but Rose's gift of her treasured
perfume . . . unless it had been that curious glow in
Daniel Wainwright's eyes after he had kissed her
fingertips.

CHAPTER 3

A WAVE OF DESPAIR WASHED OVER ABBY as she awakened the next morning. Refusing to succumb to it, she flung off her covers and padded to the window. She pulled aside the heavy draperies and was heartened to see sunshine beaming over the bright spring greenery in Union Square Park. She must concentrate upon enduring, she told herself, enduring this day, then another and another.

At her armoire, she rummaged through the dresses and felt a stab of panic. Nothing that was suitable for mourning would still fit her. She'd have to send Molly out shopping for black dresses, but if there was no money . . . A thought struck her. Her mother's rich wardrobe included a number of black dresses and she certainly would not have taken them all to Europe. But what a gruesome thought! Still, there was no money . . .

In any case, she had no choice this morning. She opened one of the trunks that Joseph had carried up to her room last night and took out another of her gray linen school frocks.

Later, when she opened her door, she half-expected to see her parents down the hallway.

"Good morning, Abby," Daniel said as he left his bedroom. "I trust you are feeling improved this morning."

"Yes, thank you."

She made an effort to concentrate on Daniel's idle conversation as they descended the staircase . . . something about the sunny May weather. Was it possible to be discussing anything as banal as the weather now?

The aromas of breakfast had already lured Uncle Benjamin to the stately dining room, where he sat drinking coffee and reading this morning's *New York Herald*. He rose to greet her. "Molly hoped that you might sleep late, but here you are ready for breakfast quite early."

"Yes."

Someone had cut fresh lilacs from the garden for a centerpiece, and their fragrance filled the room. They did not, however, change the appearance of the old oak kitchen table and chairs that formerly seated eight servants. The rough furniture looked incongruous with the marble floor, rose damask wallcoverings, and heavy draperies. The place settings were at the far end of the table, and her uncle had properly appropriated the chair at the head. He put aside the newspaper. "Did you sleep well, child?"

She bristled at the word *child*, although this morning she must look it in her school dress and with her hair pulled back into a simple knot atop her head. "I'm almost ashamed . . . I slept eleven hours."

"You needed it," Daniel said, pulling out a chair for her.

"It didn't seem right for me to be sleeping soundly under the circumstances," she replied with embarrassment.

Her uncle said, "Sleep rarely hurts anyone."

28

Daniel settled in a chair across from her, the drowsiness around his eyes bestowing a boyish appeal to his bearded face. "Now how does that go?" he asked himself. "Ah . . . 'blessings on him who first invented sleep. It covers a man all over, thoughts and all, like a cloak. It is meat for the hungry, drink for the thirsty, heat for the cold, and cold for the hot. It makes the shepherd equal to the monarch, and the fool to the wise.'"

Benjamin Talbot chuckled. "Isn't it early for Cervantes?"

"My regrets," Daniel returned with a small grin.

Abby realized that he was attempting to lift her spirits, to divert her from the onerous duties ahead. "It's astonishing for anyone to quote Cervantes so early in the morning," she said. Her parents had rarely spoken at all on those few occasions they had breakfasted together in this room.

"Don't tempt him, Abby, or we'll hear it until our brains reel. Daniel has a memory for quotations like— like—"

"An elephant?" Daniel suggested with amusement.

"More like a caged poet," Uncle Benjamin responded, smiling. "And now shall we say grace?"

Surprised, Abby sat blinking while her uncle and Daniel bowed their heads; Molly, taken unaware as well, set the coffeepot down. Abby bowed her head quickly and her uncle prayed:

Father in Heaven, from above
Look down upon this home with love.
Keep us in health and strength this day,
Give us our daily bread, we pray,
And for Thy gifts so full and free,
We would return our thanks to Thee.

"Amen," he added, and Daniel echoed a firm "Amen."

Molly poured the steaming coffee, and Daniel remarked, "I haven't heard that prayer in a long time."

"It seemed most suitable," Benjamin Talbot replied.

Abby spread the white napkin across her lap. The prayer was rather pleasant, albeit unusual in this house. She helped herself to several spoonfuls of hot porridge and poured maple syrup on it, thankful for the quiet interlude.

It wasn't until Molly removed the dishes that Benjamin Talbot said in a tone of regret, "If you like, Abby, I'll make arrangements for your parents' memorial service. I have delayed the matter so I might know your preferences."

"I–I don't know how to plan a memorial service," she said. "I've only been to Grandmother Talbot's funeral in Boston, but I hardly remember. I must have been eight or nine years old." She mainly recalled the coffin being lowered into the grave, and how she refused to throw a handful of dirt upon it. She couldn't bear to think of it any more than she could consider her parents' bodies, awash somewhere in the Mediterranean Sea. She swallowed hard. "I would appreciate your help."

"The service could be held here at the house if your parents were not members of a church," her uncle suggested. "I am not aware of how they stood, spiritually speaking."

Abby quailed at the thought. Her mother had spoken of Christian virtues and had contributed to Christian charities . . . and her father, despite his enthusiasm over transcendentalism, had allowed Mother to take her to church on Christmas and Easter. He had even accompanied them when she was very young. But in truth, even she didn't know where they had stood spiritually. Social events had meant everything to them and their friends—dinner parties, theater, concerts, balls.

She saw that her uncle awaited a reply. "I don't think we can hold a service in this—this empty house. Perhaps if you could contact the church—"

"I'll attend to it the first thing this morning," her uncle said. "Also, your parents' friends, Mr. and Mrs. Cornelius Adams, have offered to hold the wake—a reception, they called it—at their home after the service. Would that seem right?"

"Yes," Abby responded with relief. "My parents would have liked that very much since they were best friends. The Adams family lives just on the other side of Union Square, and they had always hoped that—" She stopped in horror at her near-gaffe about Cornelius and herself. "Yes," she amended, "their having the reception would be very nice."

Her uncle inquired, "Do you have suitable mourning clothing? I don't expect school uniforms will do in public."

"I-I thought that Molly and I might be able to alter some of Mother's black dresses—" her voice faltered—"and there might be some black fabric upstairs in the sewing room."

Her uncle asked Molly, who was carrying out the last of the dishes, "Will you have time to help Abby with mourning clothes?"

"Yes, Mr. Talbot. We'll be doin' it somehow."

Benjamin Talbot nodded and turned again to Abby. "I understand that you are not betrothed, but that there is a young man."

She bit down on her trembling lower lip, aware that Daniel was watching her, which made her feel oddly perverse. "Everyone said we were too young to consider any arrangement."

"I see," her uncle replied. "Unfortunately, time is running out now. Will your friend—Cornelius, I believe—will he call on you soon?"

Had Cornelius's father told her uncle about both families' expectations? "Yes, I think that Cornelius might call today. I should let him know not to come to the school musicale Saturday on my account." She shrank at the prospect of marrying Cornelius, *if* he

31

asked her. He had not even hinted at it; in fact, he had never so much as given her a romantic glance when they went horseback riding, nor held her hand when they attended plays or concerts.

"There is another matter to discuss this morning." Uncle Benjamin's brown eyes clouded with concern. "My family and I expect to emigrate to California by covered wagon next spring to expand our trading interests. If you decide to come with us—"

"Emigrate to California! But that is part of Mexico!" The idea was preposterous.

Her uncle raised an eyebrow. "Very few people know where California is. How do you?"

"We studied about Fremont's recent explorations in school. There are mountains to cross . . ."

Daniel smiled wryly. "Merely the Rocky Mountain chain and then the California Mountains. But California is a magnificent place, warm and sunny, and there are vast *ranchos* with grazing cattle as far as the eye can see."

"Yes, I remember now that you visited the Mexican Territories."

"Though I sailed around the Horn."

"Would you be going to California too?" she asked Daniel.

His blue eyes shone. "I sincerely hope so."

It was becoming abundantly clear: she must either go West or marry Cornelius. Those were her choices . . . her *only* choices. She turned to her uncle. "And when must I give you my decision?"

He took a final sip of coffee. "We'll have to know in the next few days to make travel arrangements. Monday afternoon at the latest. We leave Wednesday morning."

Wednesday! At length she said, "I see." How could she ever endure such an uprooting?

"And now if I may be excused," her uncle said, "I'll be on my way to the church."

As her uncle left the dining room, Daniel smiled warmly at her, arousing a vague contrariness. After a moment she asked, "Do you think that Uncle Benjamin wants me to be married immediately? . . . to–to encourage Cornelius?"

Daniel's smile faded. "I doubt that very much. Your uncle is as fine a man as God has ever placed on this earth. I'm sure he is only concerned with your welfare and happiness." He raised an inquisitive eyebrow. "Would you know how to encourage a man, Abby?"

His tone sounded innocent, not as if he were trying to bait her, but blood rushed to her cheeks. "Why, I don't believe that is a proper question, Mr. Wainwright!" As for its answer, the girls at school had discussed ploys to bring recalcitrant suitors to their knees, but she could not imagine using any of them. They seemed dishonest—and often ludicrous.

Daniel's color had risen as well. "Forgive me. I didn't mean it quite the way it sounded." His tone was sincere, his blue eyes regretful, as he stood awaiting her forgiveness.

"Yes, of course, you are forgiven."

"Thank you." He gave her a slight smile before starting for the library. "And please not *Mr.* Wainwright again."

She nodded and returned a small smile.

As he departed from sight, she reflected over his question: *Would you know how to encourage a man?*

When Daniel left for the banking district, she discussed the mourning clothes dilemma with Molly, who agreed to work on it immediately. It was after nine o'clock before Abby sat down again at the dining room table to write a note to Cornelius. Perhaps she should encourage him a bit, but how?

Dear Cornelius wouldn't do, she decided. She wrote sentence after sentence, then scratched them

33

out. Finally she was satisfied with what appeared to be a hastily scrawled note.

Cornelius—

    I am home and will not be at the musicale at Miss Sheffield's Saturday night. As you must know from what you have heard at the bank, I have a great many difficult decisions to make and would appreciate your assistance. May I look forward to seeing you this afternoon for tea?

Sincerely,
Abigail Talbot

She rang for Joseph to carry the note to the bank to Cornelius, and then she had no alternative to joining Molly in her parents' bedrooms.

Molly stood aside to let Abby in. Never having spent much time in her parents' suite, she was uncertain of what to expect. It only took a glance to see that the rooms were nearly empty. She started toward her mother's armoires, noting an appraisal firm's tags hanging from the hinges.

Molly remarked sadly as she opened an armoire, "There's things in life that have to be done if you want to or not."

Abby nodded, her heart constricting as she touched the beautiful morning, afternoon, and evening dresses her mother had worn. Special gowns evoked memories of her, fashionably dressed for balls, parties, and musicales, and of Father in his formal attire. They had looked so magnificent . . . so immortal with their brilliant smiles. She could remember them as though in an oil painting, her father placing the ermine wrap around her mother's shoulders. *In Society,* Abby titled it, tears clouding her eyes.

"Sure an' it's all right to cry," Molly allowed.

Abby shook her head. "No! I will not!"

Her emotions threatened to undermine her again as she tried on her mother's black dresses. There were two crepe, one bombazine, and a fine lawn—all too tight and too short, their necklines too revealing.

"They got wide seams and good hems," Molly observed, "and we'll fill in the low necks with insets. I know a bit about sewin'. We'll remake them ourselves."

"I'm afraid we have no other choice," Abby replied.

At eleven o'clock Joseph returned from his errands with an answer from Cornelius. Abby quickly tore open the envelope.

Abigail—

I shall be pleased to assist you and will call for tea this afternoon.

Sincerely,
Cornelius Adams, III

Abby sighed hopelessly. He had struck the same noncommittal tone she had used. What did he think about her situation? How did he feel about her? If only she had some notion, it might help her know what to say this afternoon.

She and Molly carried down the black dresses to the dining room table, and Abby settled down to rip stitches from the seams and hemlines. It was a shame that at Miss Sheffield's she had not learned anything terribly useful like sewing. At the moment, Latin, French, literature, elocution, art, and music were of little benefit.

Several hours later Uncle Benjamin returned. "The minister has agreed to a memorial service at the church Monday afternoon at one o'clock. How does that appeal to you, Abby?"

She was growing accustomed to the constant gnaw of anguish. "Yes, that sounds fine." Had her uncle made a point of Grandfather Talbot's ministry in Boston? Perhaps that was why they were being allowed the memorial service even though they were not members of this church. Perhaps he had even made a contribution. He had already paid her tuition, and she did not want him to spend more money for her or her parents' affairs. If only she had funds of her own!

"Mr. Cornelius Adams is callin'," Molly announced at tea time.

Abby hurried to the entrance hall and hesitated as she saw Cornelius staring at the emptiness of the place with apparent regret—or was it alarm? As usual, he was in the height of fashion in a gray coat with short tails, white high-collared shirt, black cravat, black trousers, spats, narrow pointed shoes, and black top hat in hand. He always dressed in the latest style, and she thought that had he lived in the last century, he would have looked at ease in velvet coats and breeches. Her father had once called him "a bit of a dandy."

She noticed that Cornelius had grown a pointed mustache since she had seen him at Christmas, though his flaxen hair kept it from being obvious. He looked as if he would prefer to be almost anywhere else. "How kind of you to come, Cornelius," she greeted him.

He gave a start. "Oh, I didn't hear you, Abigail!" Upon recovering, he added, "May I convey my deepest sympathies? We . . . that is, my family and I are distressed about the entire matter. If there is anything that we might do to assist you, please don't hesitate to ask."

Abby's eyes closed with anguish. "Thank you. I appreciate your parents' kindness, having the reception at your house."

"Yes . . . well, it was the very least we could do."

She hardly knew what to say into the silence that fell between them and finally ventured, "You've grown a mustache."

"Yes. Do you like it?"

"I'm not sure yet. You look so different." From an

artistic viewpoint, the mustache provided a horizontal break for his overlong face, dividing the aristocratic nose from his jutting chin. If the mustache were darker, perhaps it would be an improvement, but it was not unsightly, only a bit absurd. "Yes, I think I do like it, Cornelius," she said, stretching the truth. "It makes you look quite mature."

He gave her a careful smile, his eyes traveling down her form. "And you've grown very beautiful, if I may say so, Abigail. You have indeed grown up."

She was uncertain how to respond. Several girls at Miss Sheffield's had heard that he was making a reputation for himself as a rake since Christmas, difficult as that was to believe. Probably she should flutter her eyelashes at him or give him a coy smile. Instead she said, "Shall we go out into the garden? I haven't seen it since I came home."

Outside, they strolled along the gravel path toward the wicker furniture that overlooked the garden, where white alyssum, pink rhododendrons, and lilacs bloomed. As they seated themselves on a settee, Cornelius remarked, "It's very nice, but I do prefer a formal garden, with everything precisely in place."

Everything precisely in place! her mind echoed, finding the expression stifling. Was Cornelius the type of "gentleman" who would always expect everything precisely in place . . . including his wife? Well, she much preferred the informality of an English garden like this.

As she gazed at the garden, a hallowed aphorism of New York society occurred to her: *It takes three generations to make a gentleman*. Cornelius was the third generation of his branch of the New York Adams family. Was it possible that he was taking this distinction too literally?

From behind them Molly said, "Beggin' your pardon. I'm bringin' the tea and cake."

"Thank you, Molly."

37

The housekeeper nodded and darted an inquisitive glance at Cornelius before arranging the tea things on the table.

When Molly left, Abby poured the tea from a plain pewter pot and served a piece of the jelly-filled cake to Cornelius.

His hand brushed hers as he took his plate, and he looked up at her curiously. What was he thinking with that hooded look in his gray eyes? His new mustache made him seem a stranger.

He placed the plate with its cup of tea and cake carefully on the table, then reached for both her hands. "Abigail," he began, "under the circumstances, what are you going to do?"

She felt uncomfortable in their awkward position, wishing to extricate her hands from his clammy grip. "I don't know." Something in his eyes bespoke a special interest in her. Perhaps he intended to ask her something of importance, yet he appeared uncertain. Suddenly she had no idea how she might respond if he proposed marriage . . . though being wed to Cornelius would make her life much easier now. It was not as if their marrying were a sudden fancy; all four of their parents had encouraged it; even Rose had suggested marrying him as a perfect solution.

He shook his head. "If only it weren't such a scandal."

CHAPTER 4

"A SCANDAL? What do you mean, Cornelius—the bankruptcy?"

"That, of course, too."

"I don't understand," she said, her hands still held awkwardly in his.

His face turned quite red. "Surely you know about Roxanna Murray. It's all just come out because of her court appeal."

"No, I have never heard of her."

"I shouldn't have spoken," Cornelius said with consternation. "Please forget my indiscretion . . ."

A reason for his strange comments struck her. It must have to do with his rumored change of character. "Cornelius, are you trying to tell me that you are betrothed?"

His face grew redder, if that were possible. "Not at all. Where should you get such an idea?"

"Why, I thought that's what you were trying to tell me . . . that you were in a scandal and—" Words failed her. What then was he trying to say? Why did he continue to hold her hands so gracelessly?

39

He blinked in bewilderment, then finally said, "I heard that your uncle intends to take you to live in Missouri."

"Only for less than a year," she explained. "Next spring they are emigrating to California . . . and, oh, Cornelius, I don't—I don't want to go!"

"To California! What a preposterous notion! And they plan to take you there! Why, your father would be livid to think of you out there among savages—"

Someone cleared his throat just inside the house, and Abby saw Daniel start through the garden toward them.

Cornelius dropped her hands. "Who is that?"

"Daniel Wainwright, a friend of my uncle's. They are both staying here."

Cornelius asked, appalled, "You mean to say he is staying here in your house? That you are unchaperoned?"

"Why, Uncle Benjamin is here . . . and Molly—"

"You know quite well that Molly and Joseph live over the carriage house."

She responded with the well-modulated voice Miss Sheffield's young ladies were taught to use when provoked. "Yes. Yes, I do, Cornelius." She turned away and nodded politely to their visitor.

Daniel's blue eyes met hers with interest, and he presented them with a dazzling smile through his dark beard. "Good afternoon. Molly sent me out for tea."

Cornelius stood up with barely concealed irritation, and Abby introduced the men. They shook hands, Daniel with genuine enthusiasm. "I hope that I am not intruding."

Cornelius responded, his face still a trifle red. "The more, the merrier, as the Bard said."

Abby busied herself with serving tea to Daniel. It was impossible not to compare the two men as they sat nearby making an effort at pleasant conversation. Cornelius appeared pale and indoorish as befitted a

40

banker, whereas Daniel's face was brown and his well-trimmed dark beard and muscular physique presented an outdoorsman impression despite his urbane dark blue suit.

Why had Molly sent Daniel out? Had she seen how matters were progressing through the kitchen window? Whatever the reason, Abby felt as if she had gained a reprieve.

At supper Uncle Benjamin said, "It's unfortunate that your friend, Cornelius, had plans for the evening. I would like to make his acquaintance. What did you think of him, Daniel?"

Daniel Wainwright sat back thoughtfully. "An old family friend . . . a young gentleman who seems rather fond of Abby."

"That is not very illuminating. I had guessed as much."

Abby's words held a tinge of hopefulness. "He will call for me tomorrow afternoon and take me out for an early supper."

"Good," Benjamin Talbot said. "I look forward to meeting him. I understand that he is twenty-two years old."

Abby sat quietly, her eyes on her plate of stew, wishing that she did not feel like a porcelain doll in a shop window display. Had her mother ever felt like this when she had reached what society called a marriageable age? Probably not. "Abby, you're too sensitive," her mother had often said. "It's an unfortunate aspect of your artistic nature."

As Molly cleared away the supper things, the three of them decided to stay at the table to review the financial affairs. Her uncle excused himself to bring out the records, and Abby took up the black dress and began to rip out stitches, aware of Daniel's eyes upon her.

"Do you love Cornelius, Abby?" he inquired.

41

She closed her eyes at his perspicacity. "Does it really matter?"

"I'm sure that it does. You promise to marry for life . . . for better or for worse, through sickness and health. Forever can be a long time, even if it is only here on earth."

She felt chagrined at the direction of their conversation again and inexplicably plunged in even deeper. "Is that why you've never married? You've never been in love?"

Daniel blinked. "I presume that is the reason."

"Perhaps it's not necessary to be in love," she ventured.

"You mean it might only be expedient to marry someone?"

She nodded. "I understand that it happens."

"Oh, I'm sure it does . . . and all too often!"

"But it won't happen to you?"

"No, I'm waiting to steal fire from heaven." He chuckled at her amazed look. "You see, I think that God has one special person on earth meant for each of us. The difficulty is that most of us pursue love blindly instead of waiting to find the intended person, and that is precisely why so many marriages are far less than perfect." He paused, his blue eyes intent upon hers. "I only say this to protect you, Abby. I don't want you to rush into marriage with Cornelius or anyone else you don't love because of your circumstances."

"I see!" she replied a bit angrily. He had no right to involve himself in her decision. She should never have allowed herself to be drawn into such a conversation, and she was about to tell him so when her uncle returned with the record books. This morning, she recalled, there had been Daniel Wainwright's far too personal inquiry about whether she knew how to encourage a man . . . and now he wanted to know whether she was in love with Cornelius!

Her uncle opened the books, then he and Daniel

settled down to study the pages of debits and credits, assets and liabilities, and names of creditors who had already appealed to the bankruptcy court. Abby continued to rip stitches as the men examined the figures. At length she finished, and joined the men over the papers. Her eyes wandered over the pages, trying to make sense of it before stopping on a familiar name.

"Who is this woman, this Roxanna Murray?" Abby asked. According to the records, the woman had received substantial monthly payments and was now appealing to the court for a large settlement too . . . as if there would be any money left!

Her uncle's face turned florid. "There are some matters that are better left alone, Abby. But I am given to understand that it is a legitimate claim."

She had been agreeable about everything else, Abby thought, but now vexation rose in her throat. They were treating her as a child, and she had finished at one of the most progressive schools for young ladies in the entire country! Moreover, Cornelius had mentioned the woman's name . . . and something about a scandal. Growing more irritated by the moment she stated, "Since I am apparently losing everything, I believe that it is my right to know about this!"

Daniel replied firmly but softly, "You don't want to know this, Abby. Just let it be."

She turned from him to her uncle. "If you don't tell me who this woman is, I shall find out through the bank or the court or somehow! I'm sure that, at the very least, I can find out from Cornelius since he has already mentioned her name!"

Benjamin Talbot gazed thoughtfully down at the table, then up into her eyes. "I had hoped to avoid this, Abby, but since you are determined to find out, it is best that you find out from me. It seems that your father . . . had two families."

43

Abby asked in amazement, "My father was a polygamist?!"

Her uncle shook his head. "No, Abby, not a polygamist. He did not marry Roxanna Murray."

She was flabbergasted, although she had heard rumors of such tawdry affairs. The girls at school sometimes whispered about them. But her father . . . that was impossible! He and her mother had had a pleasant relationship, though it was true that they were rarely affectionate with each other, or with her. No—she did not want to believe it . . . yet the men's distraught expressions made it plain that this must be true. "Did they—did they have children together?"

Benjamin Talbot replied with reluctance, "Yes, they did." Her uncle gazed down at the table. "Five."

"Five children!" She rose from her chair. "What of Mother's situation in all of this?"

Daniel had uneasily risen from the table with her, and now her uncle shook his head haplessly. "According to your father, your mother dared not have any more children after you were born. She . . . she simply accepted the arrangement." He hesitated, then went on, "When I visited here ten years ago it was about this matter. Your Grandmother Talbot requested that I at least attempt to persuade your father to terminate the affair, but our suggestions were not well taken. My interference led to a rift between your father and me. You father suggested that I not visit again."

Abby exclaimed, "I refuse to believe it! It's a hoax of some kind. This—this woman is trying to extort money!" She doubted her own words as she fled from the dining room, certain only that she must vehemently deny the disgrace.

"Abby!" Daniel called behind her. He caught her by the arm in the front hallway. "Look at me, Abby," he insisted and turned her to face him, his hands gripping her shoulders.

He towered over her, his broad shoulders an impassible wall. She pressed her hands against his chest in an effort to escape, but to no avail. "Let me go!" Never had a man held her with such strength, his fingers biting through her gray school dress into her flesh. She was so bewildered to be near him, his warm breath wafting against her hair, his blue eyes full of determination, that she closed her own eyes as if that would somehow help her to avoid what he might say.

"You have to face truth, Abby," he said. "You must forgive each of them . . . your father, your mother, the woman . . . You must forgive them."

"I will never forgive any of them! Never!"

"Abby—"

She waited until his grip slackened to twist free and flee toward the stairs. Turning, she saw his disappointed expression and his failure to follow. She ran up the steps, aware of the ghostly marks on the wall where paintings of her illustrious family had once hung. *You must never do anything to shame the family name.* How had her father dared to say that! Just as furiously, she recalled her mother's constant refrain: "What will people think?"

Apparently the news about their scandal was all over the city since Cornelius knew! Everyone in New York probably knew!

She tossed her head and trudged up the remaining stairs. The revelation of her parents' duplicity was such a blow that she no longer cared about anything but leaving the house as soon as possible, leaving it all behind her. If Cornelius did perchance propose—despite this scandal—she would not even care to live in this house. As for Daniel Wainwright's insistence that she forgive them . . . they had ruined her life! No matter what Daniel Wainwright said, she would never forgive them!

CHAPTER 5

SUNSHINE STREAMED THROUGH the dining room windows and the fragrance of cut lilacs lingered about the table during breakfast on Saturday morning. Abby, Daniel, and Benjamin Talbot ate without mentioning the scandal, and she fervently hoped never to hear of it again. It was a subdued meal, during which the men occasionally eyed her with concern. Well, they need not worry—if nothing else, her fury lent her strength and determination. Moreover, Cornelius had invited her out this afternoon, and she intended to make it a turning point.

After breakfast, Daniel adjourned to the library and Uncle Benjamin departed for downtown. She'd have to speak with Daniel alone, she thought as she set about finishing the memorial service announcements. By eleven o'clock they were all written, and she handed them over to Joseph for delivery to her parents' friends.

Abby settled again at the dining room table to rework her mother's black lawn gown. If only everything would work out as well as her mourning attire solution. Money was what she needed, a great deal of it—whether she married Cornelius or not. In either event, she could not borrow from him or her uncle, who had already paid her tuition and was probably purchasing the household provisions with his own funds.

The library door opened, and she heard Daniel's approaching footsteps. It was the moment she had hoped for, the reason she had worn the pendant under her gray school dress, where it felt warm against her chest.

"Do you mind if I join you for a few minutes, Abby?" His voice was low and resonant as always. He had removed his suitcoat and cravat, and appeared at ease in his white linen shirtsleeves, fawn broadcloth vest, and dark brown trousers.

How masculine he was from his muscular shoulders and arms to his narrow waist and hips, she thought, then had to force away the memory of last night when her hands had pressed against his chest. "As a matter of fact," she responded, "I had hoped to speak with you alone."

He sat down nearby, at the head of the table, and the sunshine slanting through the windows burnished the reddish highlights in his dark brown hair and beard. "I hope that you don't intend to scold me about last night," he said uneasily. "I came to ask your forgiveness for manhandling you so."

His apology was unexpected. "Yes, of course."

He smiled briefly, his eyes still serious. "Thank you. I was so adamant about forgiving others last night because I had to learn the hard way about it myself. I hoped that it wouldn't be necessary for you to endure what I went through."

"I appreciate your concern." She hesitated, unable to broach the matter of selling the pendant, finally asking, "What is it like in Independence, Missouri?"

He raised his dark brows thoughtfully. "You might

think it somewhat primitive after New York, but I find it exciting. The wagon trains gather there for trading expeditions on the Santa Fe Trail, as do emigrants traveling to Oregon . . . and to California now. The roads are full of oxen and covered wagons, mules, horses, dogs, and an amazing variety of people. The best word to describe it might be *colorful*."

"You prefer it to New York?" she asked, incredulous.

He smiled at her astonishment. "Yes, I enjoy a great deal about the frontier. It's full of adventure . . . and west of the Kansas River, the land is a vast green prairie abloom with wildflowers . . . the sky is open and magnificent. I've only been along the trail a partway into the Indian Territory, but I think the vistas would interest you as an artist. As for New York, it's culturally edifying, but there's a crowded, stultifying feeling about it after the frontier. But you don't care for change, do you?"

"No—no, I daresay I don't."

He glanced about the spacious dining room. "After a life like yours in a fine school and living in a mansion, change can't seem appealing."

She decided to let the subject drop. The more she considered the West, the less she wanted to go. After a moment's silence she asked, "I wonder if I might ask you to do me a favor . . . something confidential."

Daniel straightened in his chair. "I'd be pleased to help in any way I'm able."

Abby reached behind her neck for the gold chain hidden under her dress, then carefully bared the sapphire pendant. "I hoped you might sell this for me."

His eyes widened at the sapphire surrounded by gold scrollwork. "It's a magnificent piece of jewelry. Are you certain that you want to sell it?"

She answered quite simply, "I have to." She feared a lecture, but at last he said, "If you must, I'll try to

48

obtain the best price. It's Saturday, so there's no possibility of my finding a buyer until Monday." He hesitated.

Her hands trembled as she unfastened the clasp behind her neck. For an instant she recalled how the stone had matched her grandmother's eyes in the old portrait, and how it had matched her dress that evening when she had descended the staircase at Miss Sheffield's school and first saw him. Her vision blurred as she quickly thrust the pendant at him.

"I'll do my best, Abby—"

"Thank you very much," she replied with a tremor in her voice and fled.

Abby picked at her midday meal in the privacy and sanctuary of her room before slipping into the altered black crepe dress. It was still fashionable with its tight long sleeves and full bell skirt; stylishness would be important to Cornelius. Molly had not yet stitched in the neckline insert, the lack of which suited Abby's purpose; she must forget how she disliked looking— wanton. Besides, her mother had often worn low necklines. Fashionable women did, and one must not make too much of it.

She studied her reflection in the mirror. If what she'd heard about Cornelius was true, he should be pleased at her womanly figure. Besides, he must realize she was no longer the girl he had been coerced by his parents into taking horseback riding and to suitable plays and musicales. She swept back her golden hair into a chignon. With her fair complexion and blue eyes she looked better than she expected in the black dress. She only hoped that Cornelius would think so too. She had made her decision: despite the scandal, she intended to remain in New York and, therefore, she must marry him.

She felt a twinge of embarrassment as she recalled Daniel's words: *Would you know how to encourage a*

49

man? She wasn't too sure, but she would have to use whatever ploys necessary to bring Cornelius around.

Abby sprayed herself liberally with *Fleur-de-lis*, pinched the pallor from her cheeks, and practiced fluttering her lashes at her reflection. She would manage it as well as she could, she promised herself, keeping an eye on the window. Molly had gone marketing and could not announce guests.

At the first glimpse of Cornelius, Abby caught up her black parasol and hurried down the staircase. To her consternation she encountered Daniel ascending the steps.

"How very . . . nice you look, Abby," he said, though he appeared stunned at her low neckline.

"Thank you," she said, lowering her eyes in embarrassment. "When Uncle Benjamin returns, please tell him that I shall not be here for supper." It was fortunate that she would not have to introduce them since her uncle might inquire about Cornelius's intentions too bluntly and frighten him off. She opened the door before Cornelius could knock.

"Well . . . Abigail!" Cornelius said, his eyes almost immediately fastening upon her decolletage. "How different you look!"

"As do you with that handsome mustache, Cornelius," she replied smoothly. "But I am growing accustomed to your mustache . . . and to your being a man now."

His fingers went to the flaxen pointed mustache, and he gave her his toothy smile. "Why, thank you, Abigail."

Stepping out the door, she added, "I do hope that you approve of . . . my growing up."

"And why shouldn't I?" His gray eyes brimmed with pleasure as he appraised her. "What a charming upstairs maid you would make in your black gown, if I may say so."

She was taken aback, then quickly rallied to tap his

50

arm playfully with her parasol before opening it. "You may, but only you! And now, my dear sir, if you'll lend an arm."

"At your service, Abigail."

She took his arm, beaming a meaningful smile at him. He did look rather attractive when he was pleased, and he wore a handsome suit, brocaded vest, and white linen shirt with the fashionable high stock around his neck. "Please call me Abby," she suggested, giving his arm a squeeze.

He blinked with astonishment. "Yes, of course . . . Abby." He belatedly remembered to close the door behind them. "I–I thought we might stroll through the park, and then hire a carriage. I didn't think that you would want to undertake anything too strenuous since you are in mourning."

"How thoughtful, Cornelius, but then you always were. I think, however, that exercise is good for me just now. At Miss Sheffield's, they have begun to encourage strenuous exercise for ladies, especially to combat distress."

"Well, then . . . we shall walk for as long as you like."

Abby had the vague impression that Daniel might be watching them from his window as they crossed the street toward the park, but she refused to allow the thought to deter her. She carried on as if this were her first outing ever with Cornelius, as if they hadn't already walked through Union Square Park scores of times. To her astonishment, her conversation issued forth as if she were an accomplished actress. Her mother had mentioned that a certain amount of illusion was required between the two sexes, a kind of haze through which men and women should not see each other too plainly. Despite her misgivings, Abby felt more and more exhilarated by her success.

After strolling through the sprawling park, they made their way to the roar and clatter of Broadway, discussing the latest concerts and plays. Later, they crossed over to Chambers Street and admired elegant shop windows displaying cut glass and silver, and fine silks and gauzes in the stores of fashion. When she married Cornelius she would certainly shop here at the great store of Mr. Alexander Stewart—when not in Paris. Marrying Cornelius would provide a number of advantages, particularly the one of staying in New York instead of living on the wild Missouri frontier.

Cornelius suggested an early supper at Astor House, the finest hotel in America, an incredible five stories high. She felt a trifle uncertain about dining in public while in mourning, but she was starved and quickly accepted.

Inside, they dined upon lobster pie, and Abby noticed several of her parents' friends passing by the table. They nodded at her, looking appalled.

"They think I am awful, already dining out," she said to Cornelius, taking the opportunity to flutter her lashes tearfully at him. "Do you think so too?"

He blinked at her coquettishness. "Not at all! It is none of their affair!"

"Thank you for being understanding, and for being so wonderful." She gazed at him soulfully, trying not to despise herself for it.

His gray eyes filled with adoration. "You are the one who is wonderful. I never really knew you before."

"Oh, Cornelius!" she protested prettily, marveling at the ardor she could arouse simply by acting and wearing a low-cut dress. She had thought him an old stick, but perhaps she had been mistaken; very likely her poor impression of him had been her own fault for giving him insufficient attention. In any event, he appeared enthralled with her now. *Young Couple Dining at Astor House*, she entitled the opulent scene, planning to sketch it soon.

As they left the dining room, she was thrilled at the

admiration she received from the waiters and other diners. Suddenly, across the room, she saw Daniel dining with two other gentlemen; he had undoubtedly been watching her for some time for he was smiling. She nodded slightly, returning a small smile, delighted that he was witnessing her success.

She and Cornelius made their way out into the warm May air through the stately columns of Astor House, Abby holding his arm as they descended the steps. Horsedrawn carriages clattered along the street, the drivers and passengers gazing with awe at the hotel and its well-dressed guests. Abby basked in their approbation, noticing that Cornelius appeared as pleased as she felt.

The liveried doorman hired a carriage from among those waiting, and Cornelius tipped the man generously. At length Abby was being helped into the cab of a fine carriage, and they rode away in elegance to the sound of their horses clip-clopping smartly through the city.

"May I?" Cornelius asked in a move to hold her hand, and, when she nodded her approval, he took it in his.

"It's not as if we haven't known each other for years," she replied, though she wished his hands were not so damp. "I don't know when I've had a finer time in my life, despite the sad circumstances, Cornelius." Her statement was true: Their outing had been most interesting; she had never before engaged in the rites of courtship.

He hesitated, then said huskily, "Abby, you know that our parents had always hoped we might be more than friends."

"Yes?" she encouraged, drawing closer to him.

His gray eyes darted toward the driver's back, then out the windows. With a look of wildness he slipped his arm around her, gathering her up to him. "I don't like the idea of your going West . . . or of leaving New

York at all. I should like to discuss it further with my family," he began, "but—"

She lifted her face to his. "Yes, my dear Cornelius?"

"Oh, Abby, I love you!" His face tilted to hers, his mustache brushing her mouth, then his wet lips settled ravenously upon hers.

She surrendered to his passion, although it was beyond her comprehension how Rose and the other girls at school enjoyed this. Perhaps she—and Cornelius—did not yet understand the art of kissing. Perhaps with time improvement would come. When he finally backed away from her, Abby realized that the carriage had stopped in front of her house.

"I love you, Abby," Cornelius uttered again. "I love you, and I will not permit you to go West."

"Oh, Cornelius," she whispered with a flush of success, "you are so wonderful."

The driver turned, leaving Abby no way to continue while Cornelius helped her out. She bid him a coquettish farewell at the door, feeling a twinge of apprehension, and, inside the house, she inexplicably burst into tears.

CHAPTER 6

THE NEXT MORNING AFTER BREAKFAST, Abby tried to avoid attending church with Daniel and her uncle, but Benjamin Talbot said, "After all, they are giving the memorial service for your parents tomorrow, even though they were not regular members."

"Yes, of course, Uncle Benjamin," Abby said, yielding.

Her uncle added, "Molly says that she has finished alterations on a suitable black dress."

Abby glanced at Daniel to see whether he had betrayed her about wearing the decolletage yesterday, but his expression remained unreadable.

Later, she arrived downstairs in her black bonnet and the black lawn frock. Molly had snipped fabric from the full skirt to fill in the bodice and sewn buttons to the top of the neck.

"You look very presentable," her uncle said.

"Thank you, Uncle Benjamin." She dared not look at Daniel again.

Her uncle continued, "This morning we received an invitation for a quiet dinner after church from the

Adams family. Since they have been kind enough to have the reception tomorrow afternoon, I accepted the invitation for all of us."

Abby's spirits soared. "How kind of them." That meant Cornelius had already spoken to his family. Perhaps there might even be an announcement of their intentions this afternoon! She supposed that Cornelius would first have to ask her uncle for her hand in marriage—

Daniel opened the door for her, smiling pleasantly.

Outside, the sky had clouded over, but even impending rain could not discourage her. As she stepped into the carriage, it occurred to her that Cornelius sometimes had to accompany his mother to church, and that they might also be in attendance.

After a short ride to the elegant church with its stained glass windows and carillon tower, Daniel helped her down from the carriage and inquired, "Did you have a pleasant dinner last evening?"

"Yes. Yes, I had a fine time, thank you. I trust that you did too."

He smiled ruefully, his hand under her elbow. "Pleasant enough, but I suspect it wasn't as fine as yours." He smelled clean, of soap, and pleasantly masculine.

His nearness unnerved her, and she quickly moved away, trying to focus on his comment. He probably meant that he had been dining with men whereas she had been part of a couple. No appropriate reply occurred to her, and she turned to look about as Joseph drove the carriage across the cobblestones.

The church bells rang out, their deep tones drifting through the misty morning air as the worshipers converged upon the Gothic gray stone edifice. Around them horses and carriages clattered away after letting out parishioners in their fine Sunday attire. A flurry of subdued greetings surrounded them, and Abby looked hopefully about for Cornelius and his mother.

Inside, the nave of the church rose skyward in a great arc and soft organ music wafted over the crowd in the wooden pews. Abby followed an usher to a pew in the middle of the sanctuary, seeing no sign of Cornelius along the way. She sat down between Daniel and her uncle, and after smoothing her black skirt, scrutinized the magnificent stained-glass windows. The one nearest them depicted Christ, arms widespread with welcome; the words inscribed below it were *I am the way, the truth, and the life*. She regarded His stained-glass eyes; it seemed for an instant that He was looking into her soul.

She quickly glanced away to her program and read, *Commit thy way unto the Lord; trust also in him; and he shall bring it to pass. Psalm 37:5*. She read the verse again. It sounded uplifting, but what did it mean? As always when she attended church, she felt on the edge of a vast mystery.

Hymnbook pages rustled as the organ began the prelude. Beside her Daniel and Uncle Benjamin rose with the congregation, and she quickly put her question aside and stood. Daniel shared his hymnal with her, singing out with the others in his deep, resonant voice,

O worship the King, all glorious above,
And gratefully sing His power and His love;
Our Shield and Defender, the Ancient of Days,
Pavilioned in splendor, and girded with praise.

A shiver coursed through her, and she sang along softly about His might and His grace. What did it mean—His robe is the Light? How peculiar that she, a minister's granddaughter, did not even know or understand the songs of the church with the exception of Christmas carols. And why had her father turned from Christianity? To be fashionable? So that he might keep a—a mistress? What disgrace *he* had brought upon himself and upon the family name through his life! She tried to put her anger aside, to concentrate on the last verse.

57

Frail children of dust, and feeble as frail,
In Thee do we trust, nor find Thee to fail;
Thy mercies how tender, how firm to the end,
Our Maker, Defender, Redeemer, and Friend.

Our Friend? What did it mean, our Friend? She
supposed that she vaguely believed in God, a faraway
God, who had made the universe, and it struck her as
odd to consider Him a friend. Her eyes went to the
nearby stained-glass window of Christ, then quickly
turned away.

She sat down with the congregation again, glancing
at Daniel, who appeared as intent upon the service as
he had been fervent in song. His inner strength
seemed to pervade the space around him. Did he
receive that peculiar quality from his faith? Her mind
went back to the morning he had spoken about his
having to forgive; something dire must have happened
to him once. Finally she forced her mind to the
sermon, which bore the rather lengthy title of "Come
unto me, all ye that labour and are heavy laden."

The pastor repeated the title words, then added
with feeling, "and I will give you rest."

Abby's lips quivered at the thought of receiving rest
from her tribulations. She was indeed heavy laden
now with the death of her parents, the bankruptcy,
the scandal, the problem of leaving New York if she
didn't marry Cornelius . . . not to mention being torn
from Miss Sheffield's before graduation and having to
give up her childhood home. She firmed her resolve.
She would not leave New York! Tears clouded her
eyes. Her parents would want her to remain here. She
felt in her pocket for a handkerchief, but it was empty.

Beside her, Daniel handed her his neatly folded
handkerchief, and she blinked gratefully at him before
dabbing her eyes, wishing that she did not cry so often
now.

"My yoke is easy, and my burden is light," the
pastor said.

What did it mean? All she knew was that her burden seemed exceedingly heavy now . . . and that something within her yearned to understand more clearly about God. Yet it was all too mysterious. Did the people here in this church understand? Did Daniel and her uncle understand what it was all about?

At length the congregation sang a solemn hymn and then remained standing. The pastor's hand reached powerfully out above the people as he blessed them, and Abby did feel as if her burdens were slightly lessened.

There was still no sign of Cornelius when they left the church, and she could only think that tomorrow they would attend her parents' memorial service here. She bit down on her trembling lips aware that people all around looked at her with sympathy . . . and that she did not want it!

Outside, Joseph awaited them with the carriage and, by the time they had driven back to Union Square Park, Abby had her emotions under control again. This dinner with Cornelius's parents and grandmother would determine the course of her life. She fervently hoped that his grandmother, who held the family purse strings, would not be as cold and formal as usual.

The Adams mansion on the opposite side of the park, though nearly twice the size of their own, was also of brownstone and equally plain on the exterior.

When the butler showed them in, however, the riches of the Adams family were evident in the fine old Italian paintings, French crystal chandelier, and Brussels carpets on the white marble of the entrance hall. The butler escorted them into the equally sumptuous green drawing room, where Cornelius and his father rose from the Venetian antique furniture to greet them. His mother and corpulent grandmother nodded graciously as the introductions to Daniel and Benjamin were made.

Abby's eyes darted to Cornelius for reassurance, but his gaze avoided hers. He was being careful, she told herself. His aloofness was simply good manners for this somber occasion. She noted that he and his entire family had worn black. *Society in Mourning*, she titled the scene of them against the drawing room's green opulence.

Cornelius's mother said, "How splendidly you are managing, Abigail. How proud of you your dear mother would be."

Abby caught a breath. "Thank you. We appreciate your kindness in having the reception here tomorrow after the memorial service."

"It was the least we could do," she replied gently.

Cornelius's father helped to seat Abby. His hooded gray eyes, so similar to his son's, surveyed her figure quite openly, as if to discover what Cornelius might see in her.

Embarrassed, Abby turned to Cornelius's grandmother, whose late husband had been president of the bank. Abby's spirits sank even lower. The enormously fat woman, whose black crepe gown did nothing to enhance her appearance, scrutinized her icily.

Abby reminded herself that the older woman was a great arbitrator in New York society, and finally managed, "It is a pleasure to see you again, Mrs. Adams."

The old dowager's gray eyes flashed like silver. "Indeed!" she replied with disbelief.

The butler stood by to take orders for refreshments, and the woman's attention turned to him. Beside them, the men had struck up a conversation. After a decent interval, Abby excused herself to freshen up. Cornelius's mother departed from the drawing room with her, chatting about the weather as if everything were quite normal. However, in the dressing room Mrs. Adams said, "Cornelius has told us about your mutual feelings, my dear. You must notice that he is being circumspect. The fact is that his grandmother feels that the two of you are quite young."

Abby stared at her in dismay. "But he is twenty-two, and I am seventeen now. It is not at all too young—"

"Yes, dear, perhaps I should have mentioned that there is more to it. Cornelius will probably not have an opportunity to tell you of his grandmother's wishes. She would prefer that he . . . marry someone else."

"Someone else! But then I must go on to Missouri!"

The auburn curls around his mother's face bobbed slightly as she nodded, and her brown eyes filled with dismay. "You know I would like to help my best friend's daughter . . . if there were only a way."

Heartsick, Abby turned to the mirror with the excuse of trying to smooth her chignon. Her voice faltered. "It is the scandal about that—that woman then, isn't it?"

"No," Beatrice Adams said, "although it is the excuse used." A trace of bitterness entered her voice. "A good many husbands in New York society have a 'friend' like your father's. When all is said and done, the problem is your family's finances. In the mind of most people, losing one's money is the real sin, although they would never say it. They can't bear to consider such a possibility for themselves."

"I see," Abby replied bleakly.

Later, in the ornate dining room, she was seated between Daniel and her uncle, leaving no opportunity for a private word with Cornelius. Perhaps he would elope with her! Perhaps that was why he was being so careful now to be distant! Yes, that must be it. She managed to catch his eye from across the table, and he nodded with what was surely more than mere politeness. Recently, more and more couples in

Society had eloped. The girls at school said it took considerable daring.

The dinner courses dragged on with dreary magnificence, and Abby held fast to her golden hope. Something would work out yet. Somehow she would be able to stay in the city. She and Cornelius would solve this dilemma!

Finally the dinner came to its elegant finale, and it was time to leave. In the entrance hall, Cornelius slipped her a note, which she quickly concealed in her pocket. She tried not to beam too broadly at the flash of passion in his eyes. He had worked something out after all!

All the way home in the carriage, she held her pocket shut, feeling warmed by the note in it. When they arrived at the Talbot mansion, she excused herself and rushed to her room. She breathlessly read Cornelius's words.

Dearest Abby, he began, and her heart quickened at the endearment. *It is said that love will find out the way. It is said too that the course of true love never did run smoothly. We are star-crossed lovers like Romeo and Juliet, but we were never meant to give up. Come out to your garden at nine o'clock tonight, my love. Adoringly, Cornelius.*

Her spirits soared again. It was as though he had read her thoughts during dinner. If he were inviting her out for a tryst tonight, he meant that they should elope!

At nine o'clock, Abby tiptoed down the steps, a small traveling bag in hand. Her uncle and Daniel had retired to their rooms, if not to bed, and she worried that they might hear. It was not an easy matter to think of eloping on the eve of her parents' memorial service, but no one would expect it of them tonight — which did make it an especially brilliant plan. She wended her way out through the kitchen, hiding her traveling bag near the door. Molly and Joseph were certain to be in their quarters over the carriage house.

The kitchen door emitted a soft squeak as she opened it and stepped out into the moonlight. She closed the door quietly and, avoiding the pale gravel path, stayed to the shadows, straining to hear his voice. Then there he was, stepping out of the darkness.

"Abby," he whispered and she ran to him, throwing herself into his arms.

"Oh, Abby!" he breathed warmly into her hair, "I knew you would come. If only you felt my anguish at dinner. If only you knew how I yearned to have you in my arms!"

His kisses were wetter than ever, but the enchantment of their moonlit tryst caused her to tremble, and the fragrance of lilacs nearly made her swoon.

"Abby, I love you," he whispered, his breath warm.

"Oh, Cornelius!" she whispered in reply, unable to vow that she truly loved him too. Love would come with time after they were married, and she would do her very best to be a good wife if he would only marry her and keep her in New York.

He kissed her forehead, her mouth, her throat. "My dearest . . ."

This, then was what it was to be in love; this was what Rose and her friends at school had intimated was so wonderful. Abby felt a twinge of disappointment, but was determined to overcome it. She *must* love him, she must! she told herself. At the very least, she must pretend!

Cornelius's kisses grew more passionate until at length he whispered, "Abby, my dearest, how much do you love me?"

Abby leaned away at the calculating tone in his voice. How much did she love him? How *much?* "Why . . . enough to have packed my bag to elope with you."

His voice filled with astonishment. "To elope?"

"But isn't that why you meant me to meet you here?"

He failed to answer her question, instead whispering, "Kiss me, Abby! Kiss me! Show me how much you love me!"

She ducked her head, reminded that the girls at school had called him a rake. Had she been wrong? Didn't he mean to elope? "You don't plan to marry me at all, do you?"

"You know that's impossible now," he whispered insistently. "You must see how my grandmother feels about it. It's simply a matter of waiting, of time to let the scandal die down. Let's not speak of it now . . . only kiss me, Abby."

He simply meant to take advantage of her situation! She was positive of it. His renewed hold on her seemed unbreakable, but she gathered her strength and, with a mighty effort, stamped her high-heeled slipper onto his toes.

He howled, rearing back and loosening his grip on her, and Abby twisted away, gathering up her skirts, and ran.

"You are a cad, Cornelius!" she shouted behind her out into the night, not caring in the least that Miss Sheffield's young ladies were to speak in well-modulated voices. "You are an unspeakable, unspeakable cad!"

Worst of all, she reflected as she let herself into the kitchen and locked the door, she had been just as terrible in her own selfish way—leading him on! Now all was lost!

CHAPTER 7

ABBY'S MOOD WAS AS MOURNFUL as her black dress, cloak, and bonnet. She arrived with Daniel and her uncle at the North River, where Daniel handed her down from the carriage onto the wharf at Pier Two, his dark brows knit with concern.

She was scarcely aware of the early morning bustle about them, only that their trunks were being directed to the ferryboat, and that she was leaving New York, perhaps forever . . . and that she must not cry. She had contained her grief all through the memorial service and the reception, even upon leaving her home this morning.

"Chin up," Daniel urged.

She nodded, tired of summoning up courage.

"It will be an adventurous journey, you'll see." His hand was at her elbow as he and Uncle Benjamin escorted her toward the ferryboat.

People swarmed around them in the sunshine— stevedores shouldering trunks and rolling heavily laden barrows over the wooden planks of the pier, peddlers hawking their wares, passengers chattering excitedly on their way to and from nearby boats. Underscoring the cacophony was the steady lapping of the North River against the sturdy pilings. The tang of salt air mingled with the pungent aromas of hot pitch, sun-dried hemp ropes, bales of tobacco, and the pervasive smell of fish. She had been rigid with anguish since awakening, but now the sounds and the smells, the tootling of boats and excited voices and bustle began to pique her interest.

"You'll be feeling better soon," Daniel remarked as they strode up the ferryboat's gangplank.

She smiled, albeit wanly, for what must have been the first time in days. "Yes, I do feel . . . better." Torment at the loss of her parents still gnawed at her, but not quite so achingly with Daniel nearby. He and her uncle had remained at her side throughout the memorial service and the dignified reception afterward. Even Cornelius had pretended that nothing unseemly had transpired between them that night, and his grandmother's absence from the reception was blamed upon illness. Both Uncle Benjamin and Daniel had appeared pleased that she evidenced no interest in marrying Cornelius.

Daniel remarked, "I would like to see you sketch a wharf scene like this, Abby, though it's doubtless rather raucous for a young lady of your upbringing." He arched a brow at her speculatively. "Could you portray it?"

He had been genuinely impressed at how determinedly she'd sketched Union Square Park, her home, and the garden yesterday morning to add to her portfolio. She glanced out over the tumult around them. "I don't know. There's so much activity and excitement." She recalled his mentioning the spirit of adventure on the frontier, and despite her sorrows and fears, she began to feel unexpected stirrings of adventure herself.

Once they were settled on one of the wooden

benches on the deck of the ferryboat, Daniel placed upon her lap the large but narrow package he had insisted upon carrying aboard himself. "For you," he said.

"Open it," he urged.

Still astonished at his gift to her, she untied the string and removed the brown paper to discover a sturdy tan leather case. She unlatched the case and opened the hinged lid. "Why, it's a portable painting case! I've never seen anything quite like it!" The case contained sketch pads, pencils, brushes, a good selection of colors, and even a collapsible easel. "I don't know how to thank you."

"Your using it will be thanks for me," he replied. "I thought you might like to draw your way to Missouri. Sights cry out to be captured, sights that will disappear as surely as the wilderness will someday. It would be a favor to everyone if you'd paint them, especially to Aunt Jessica and the rest of the family in Missouri. Most of them may never have the privilege of traveling through the places you will see."

"Yes—I hadn't thought of that." It *would* keep her mind occupied. "But I'm not sure I can do such scenes justice."

Her uncle said, "No matter how you depict them, your drawings would be the finest gift you could ever bring to my family. They are unfailingly curious about the sights I see on my trade expeditions."

"Then I can at least attempt it," she decided aloud. "You have both been so good to me." Her mouth trembled, and she closed it firmly to regain her composure.

Daniel suggested, "Why don't you start now, Abby?"

She looked up at him, realizing that she enjoyed the sound of her name from his lips. At the concern in his eyes, she quickly turned her attention to the pencils. "Yes, perhaps I shall." She opened a sketch book and took up a pencil. After a moment's deliberation, she began to lightly sketch the scene at Pier Two of the North River: the wharfside color and excitement, the ferries, skiffs, rafts, and elegant packets plying the swiftly flowing water. She would have to remember the precise colors and shadings to add later, perhaps when she arrived in Independence.

Daniel said, "You might call it *Tumult at North River.*"

"Yes . . . *Tumult at North River.*" Pleased at his interest, her pencil moved with greater sureness. His title suited the sketch taking shape before her, implying new beginnings . . . forward movement through tumult, no matter what happened.

While the ferryboat steamed across the water and Daniel and her uncle strolled about the deck, she rapidly sketched the vistas up and down the North River and along its New York and New Jersey banks, everything she could see of the panorama in the clarity of the sun's radiance.

As they stepped into their railroad car Uncle Benjamin said, "You two take that seat together. I'll sit up there." He waved toward the other vacant seat near the front.

Abby obediently headed for the empty double seat by the window, noting Daniel's perplexed glance at her uncle. After they had settled themselves, he extracted the morning's *New York Herald* from his black leather valise. The two of them had spent little time alone except in brief discussion of the generous amount of money he had obtained for her sapphire pendant. She had insisted on using some of the money to pay her way to Independence; Daniel would accompany her to deposit the rest in a bank when he joined them in Independence.

The locomotive blasted a throaty warning, emitting a cloud of steam, and the conductor called out, "All aboard! New Brunswick! Trenton! Philadelphia!'' The train blasted another warning before the doors were slammed shut and the cars jerked into motion along the track. Abby gripped the armrest near the window, peering out at the Jersey City railroad station. White steam from the locomotive billowed forth as they chugged into the New Jersey countryside.

Daniel had opened his newspaper, but he was apparently unable to concentrate on it, for he asked, "Is this your first train ride?"

"At Miss Sheffield's we sometimes went on short excursions." The truth was that she had very little railroading experience; her parents had rarely taken her along on their travels. Moreover, his tone of voice had implied that she was quite young. She cast a glance at him and found him gazing at her rather tenderly.

She quickly took up the portable drawing case.

"Here, let me help you," he offered, and there was nothing to do but allow him to set the case across their knees, then for her to extract pencils and sketch pad, and thank him.

"My pleasure," he responded, closing the case. He leaned across her to prop it up under the window. She was suddenly aware again of his clean masculine smell and he must have been equally aware of her since he commented, "You smell of flowers, rather like a spring garden."

"It—it's *Fleur-de-lis*. My best friend at school gave it to me for my birthday . . . before I left."

"I'm sorry. Your uncle and I didn't know. Even if we had . . . well, it wasn't a suitable day for birthday festivities, was it?"

"No. I daresay it wasn't."

"How old are you, Abby?"

Oh, why must he ask!

He chuckled. "Are you going to inform me again that it's impolite to ask such questions?"

69

She gave a little laugh. "Yes. It is not polite to ask."

He sat back against his seat with an enigmatic smile spreading across his lips. "You are seventeen years old."

"Really, that's unfair! You might at least have guessed eighteen since most of the girls in my class at Miss Sheffield's were."

Amusement danced about his lips, and she suddenly wanted to touch them, to run her fingers through the waves of his neatly-cropped beard. If only he weren't leaving her and Uncle Benjamin in Philadelphia!

His expression turned serious and he reached for her hand, extracting the sketching pencil from it. His eyes held hers, darkening with ardor as he brought her fingertips to his warm lips. Her heart pounded so furiously that she was sure he could hear it. He hesitated, then said, "You are far too beautiful for your own good, Miss Abigail Talbot. But I presume you have heard that before."

Her heart leapt. "You are the first man who has ever said so."

His eyes sparkled. "Well, I am glad of that!"

Despite all of his questions and teasing, he did care for her! He was holding her hand in his! Wonder unfolded within her. *I love him,* she thought. *I love him. I love Daniel Wainwright!*

His color rose. "You must never look at a man like that, Abby." He appeared disconcerted, and he replaced the sketching pencil in her hand. "Here, better get to work before—"

"Before what?"

"Before you . . . lead me on any further!" he replied with an uncertain laugh.

She flushed furiously and turned toward the window, aware that he was opening his newspaper again. He could read her thoughts as easily as he read the newspaper! What must he think? He had held her hand, even kissed her fingertips again . . . and he had seen bits of the drama she had played with Cornelius. Perhaps Daniel thought that she was always like this with men. What if he did not approve of her? And what if Uncle Benjamin's family did not approve of her either?

Calming herself, she set about sketching the New Jersey countryside in its spring green as the train rushed past. When she had completed several rough sketches, she noticed that Daniel had finished with the newspaper, and she ventured, "I'm afraid I'm a bit nervous about moving in with Uncle Benjamin and his family. I–I wonder how they will accept me, a complete stranger, particularly since our families were not close."

"You can put any such anxieties to rest," Daniel assured her. "They will accept you with great open hearts as they did me." He studied her countenance, then said, "Perhaps you should know how I came to be part of their family. I'm sure that you'll eventually find out—not that they would be the ones to tell you."

"I only know that they took you in as a child. It didn't seem my place to inquire beyond that."

"Then it is my place to tell you." He gazed past her out the train window thoughtfully. "It started when I was five years old and moving to Missouri with my parents by covered wagon. We had stopped for the night, down by a creek, and I was sent out to find firewood. I looked about for wood for quite a while and, as I returned . . . I saw three Indians approaching the covered wagon. I was so frightened that I hid behind a tree." He drew a regretful breath. "To make a short story of it, the Indians killed my family."

"How terrible! How terrible for anyone . . . and for a little boy!"

"It certainly was." He closed his eyes for a

71

moment. "I saw it. Rather, some of it. I was still shaking in terror behind that tree when they came out into the open carrying my mother's and father's scalps."

"Oh, Daniel!"

"I was shocked, then full of terror and rage and grief. I became filled with hatred toward all Indians. I might never have come out of it sane if your uncle hadn't found me there trying to bury my parents. I know now that it was not by coincidence that he came. At any rate, he took me in . . . he and your Aunt Elizabeth, who was still alive then, and they raised me as if I were one of their own children."

Abby stammered, "I–I had no idea, but then I know so little about you . . . or about Uncle Benjamin and his family."

"They were wonderful to me. And now we arrive at why I was so adamant that night about your having to forgive your parents and Roxanna Murray . . ."

"I went through years of agony," he continued, "nightmares by night and flashes of the memory by day. I finally learned that we must totally forgive others and ourselves, just as God will forgive us if we ask."

She gazed blindly out the window. "You spoke of an uncle in Boston. Why didn't you live with him?"

"At that age, I only knew that my father had an older brother back East. He finally found me when I was fourteen, and he had me educated in Boston, with your cousin, Adam, who is my age. Later, I entered the shipping and chandlery firm owned by my uncle, Elisha Wainwright, who is a childless widower. Daniel furrowed his brow. "I rarely tell anyone about that childhood experience, but I wanted you to understand why I spoke so strongly about your forgiveness that night. I don't want you to endure more grief."

"Thank you for your concern," she said, quickly

72

turning to her sketching again. She did not intend to dwell on the scandal; as far as she was concerned, that was over. She intended to forget that she had even heard about it—to simply forget! True, Daniel had survived a terrible hardship, and it had given him strength. Well, Abigail Windsor Talbot would survive the hardships of life too—but in her own way!

Daniel dozed from New Brunswick to Trenton, and Abby sketched him, her pencil caressing the soft curls of his hair and beard, his long dark eyelashes resting against his cheeks. His nose was straight, his forehead high, his neck thick and strong. She quickly drew in his broad shoulders. Now that she knew more about his background she was able to capture not only his aura of strength, but the surprising tenderness about his lips, the fine smile lines near his eyes.

Suddenly he gazed up at her. It was an instant before he realized why she was looking at him, and he straightened up in his seat. "Are you drawing a portrait of me?"

"Yes. I hope you don't mind."

Peering down at his likeness, he raised an interested brow. "I don't look like that when I sleep, do I?"

"I thought so. Maybe I shouldn't have . . . drawn it." She fought the color rising to her cheeks. Didn't he know what a handsome man he was? She closed her sketch pad, hoping that he would not demand the portrait.

"What do you intend to do with it?" he inquired.

"I–I thought I'd keep it with the others of this journey to share with your family—*Daniel Sleeping through New Jersey.*"

He smiled. "Well, I'm certain that they have seen me looking far worse."

In truth, she did not want to share the drawing with anyone. Her fascination with him was obvious in its every pencil stroke.

CHAPTER 8

It was nearly nightfall when they arrived in Philadelphia. In the rainy grayness, Abby felt more saddened to think of leaving Daniel behind than she was of being deprived of a tour of the cosmopolitan city.

Daniel quoted a British writer's description of the major eastern cities. "Boston turns up her erudite nose at New York; Philadelphia, in her pride, looks down upon both New York and Boston; while New York, chinking her dollars, swears the Bostonians are a parcel of puritanical prigs, and the Philadelphians a would-be aristocracy."

"Precisely!" Benjamin Talbot agreed with a laugh. "Pride makes fools of us all."

Sitting between them in the carriage, Abby was not nearly so interested in civic pride as she was in the growing intensity between her and Daniel.

Now her uncle gazed with disappointment out the carriage window at the dreary weather. "I suppose we will have to take dinner at the hotel and stay in. I had hoped that we might have a stroll around the city."

Abby had no idea how the three of them might be accommodated, but at the Philadelphian Hotel the men arranged for a suite with a small sitting room and two bedrooms, one for her, and the other for them. Once they were installed, she removed her bonnet and changed from the black traveling dress to the more elegant black bombazine. It was a relief to brush her hair, to sweep it up anew, allowing a few blonde tendrils to curl on her forehead and about her ears. When she returned to the sitting room, Daniel's eyes filled with approval at her appearance, and her heart lifted with happiness. Even Uncle Benjamin said, "You look very presentable, Abby; but then you always do."

Downstairs, the hotel dining room's lack of opulence seemed insignificant in Daniel's company. It mattered little whether the chandeliers were French or the carpeting Persian; nor was it of import to dine upon lobster pie. She was more than content with her roast beef dinner with its spring potatoes, gravy, and fresh peas.

Whenever Daniel caught her eye, she felt a surge of bittersweet joy. They would part in the morning, but she would sketch these precious moments to remember him.

After dinner, Benjamin Talbot excused himself. "You two stay for dessert. An old fellow like me has to get his sleep before attempting the portage railroad tomorrow."

The men had discussed the vagaries of the upcoming crossing of the Allegheny Mountains with amusement, but it sounded precarious to her. As her uncle made his way through the dining room she said, "Perhaps I should retire now."

Daniel caught her hand in his on the table. "Not just yet. Fresh strawberries and cream, Abby?"

"Yes, that would be fine."

A radiance glowed between them, and it was as

though they were alone in the vast dining room, uninterrupted by their waiter's comings and goings. Their words flowed with ease—where strawberries might come from so early in the year, what a pleasant hotel the Philadelphian was with its subdued chandeliers and fine table linen and silver. The words meant nothing—nothing mattered except their being encircled by this wonderful glow. She did not require decollete to attract Daniel, nor did she need to pretend as she had with Cornelius. This palpable glow was elemental, drawing them together like moths to gaslight. After he signed for dinner, she was vaguely aware that they were wending their way through the dining room, then seemingly floating up the hotel's staircase to the suite.

In the hallway Daniel unlocked the door, and she stepped into the dimly lit sitting room, waiting . . . waiting for she knew not what.

Closing the door behind them, he gazed at her for a long moment, then they were in each other's arms. "Abby!"

Her lips were eager for his. *Oh, Daniel . . .* her heart cried, her mouth returning the pressure of his warm lips. As if at their own volition, her arms slipped up over his shoulders, her fingertips into the curls at the nape of his neck. His lips were tender upon hers, tentative and searching, then firming with passion. She felt no twinges of disappointment with him, only a luminescent bliss.

After a long while Daniel moved away, gently removing her hands from behind his neck. In the flickering light, she saw his anguish. "I'm sorry," he finally said. "I'm sorry, Abby. I shouldn't have presumed . . . you are so terribly young."

"I'm seventeen, Daniel. Not so very young."

He shook his head. "Again, please forgive me."

"I don't want to forgive you!" she said with yearning. "I want you to kiss me again!"

"Oh, Abby—" he protested, then acquiesced, kissing her until she was breathless. At length he held her away again. "Good night, Abby."

Tremulous, she asked, "Do you think that I'm wanton?"

He smiled, his teeth white against his beard in the dimly lit sitting room. "No. Only very innocent and . . . very desirable."

"Desirable?" she repeated with uncertainty.

"Very lovable," he amended, "and that is why we must say good night now. You—you must be more careful around men."

She finally returned his smile, appreciating his concern. "Good night then, Daniel."

In her room she thought she might never fall asleep—remembering his embrace, his lips upon hers. Whatever caused his restraint could be overcome, she decided as she slipped into her bed. He had said she was very lovable! She lay glorying in the wonder of their love until she drifted into a sleep filled with dream after dream of him.

The next morning, she hurriedly repacked for the trip to Pittsburgh. Daniel was quiet at breakfast, preoccupied, yet when he gazed at her at the railroad station his expression turned exceedingly tender. She yearned for another kiss, but had to be content with the love in his eyes and his gallant kiss upon her fingertips. "Goodbye, Abby," he said, his voice again making her name unbelievably beautiful.

As the train left Daniel far behind at the station, her eyes clouded, and she surreptitiously touched the fingers he had kissed to her lips.

My dearest friend, Rose,

I am writing aboard a steamboat, the Columbia, *which in some aspects is not unlike New York's floating palaces in magnificence. It is new and the finest boat we have seen on the river. My uncle, Benjamin Talbot, and I embarked in Pittsburgh and have been steaming along* the Ohio River for some days. You will be pleased to know that I am sketching enroute. In the evenings I add the watercolors in my stateroom.

Matters did not work out between Cornelius and me, and now that I am on this adventure, I am not too sorry. Daniel Wainwright—the one you thought so romantic with his beard and "eyes the color of the sea at Marblehead"—presented me with a portable painting case when we departed from New York. Just writing Daniel's name induces a wonderful glow of love—yes, I am smitten—but I fear that he thinks me too young. Worse, I shall not see him for months as he will be in Philadelphia, Boston, and New York.

It took over three days to reach Pittsburgh, where we boarded the Columbia. What sights we see as we steam along the Ohio River! Last week we noticed a procession of people moving from a village toward the river. At first no one understood their intentions. Finally one of the men left the others standing on the bank and walked into the river with a woman dressed in black. They stood motionless, then suddenly he submerged her backward into the water! A baptism! Can you imagine it! I titled my sketch of the scene Frontier Baptism—far too unpoetic. Perhaps Daniel will think of a better title.

A spirit of adventure abounds along the river. Between Cincinnati and Louisville, we saw the mail packet grounded on a sandbank; it had already been there for a day despite their hard work to float free. No wonder that letters to and from the frontier take so long!

Frontier people are a hardy lot. A typical steamboat breakfast includes beefsteak, chicken fricassee, all the pancakes one can eat, and for finicky eaters, "Baptized Toast," which we called milk toast at school. The men seem a much rougher lot than those in our social circles in New York, but they unfailingly treat me like a lady, perhaps because I wear mourning. The women are abustle with children; many our age have two or three!

In St. Louis, I hope to see John Charles Fremont and his famous guide, Kit Carson, who are preparing for another expedition into the Far West. Those aboard discuss the explorations, and the newspapers insist "Our manifest destiny is to overspread this continent." It

78

*sounds exciting, but I cannot reconcile myself to going to
California, and often hope that something might hold me
in Independence or even bring me back to New York.*

*How I miss you, my dear friend, and cherish your gift
of* Fleur-de-lis, *knowing how much it meant to you. I
think that Daniel too enjoyed its lovely fragrance. How
daring that sounds! What would Miss Sheffield say?*

*You must be in the final preparations for your wedding
now, and I send my fondest wishes. I am so sorry that I
cannot attend. When I am able, I will ship a special
wedding gift from the frontier. Now I can only send my
love, which I do most heartily.*

> *Your loving friend,*
> *Abby*

*P.S. Please write me in care of my uncle: Benjamin
Talbot, Independence, Missouri. He assures me that it is
not necessary to use a street address!*

Abby posted the letter in St. Louis, where the
streets bustled with carriages, buggies, drays, oxcarts,
and covered wagons, the sidewalks were crowded
with a vast array of people—riverboat gamblers,
dance hall women, traders readying for the Santa Fe
Trail, harried clerks, bullwhackers seeking jobs with
wagon trains, fur traders from the mountains, merchants loading goods on Missouri River boats. In the
hustle and bustle she did not see John Charles
Fremont or Kit Carson; it was a wonder her uncle
found his business associates in the fray.

Two days later, they left on a squat steamboat and
traveled the twisting 250 miles westward on the
muddy Missouri River. Their boat carried a cargo of
flour, whiskey, sugar, and iron castings, and Uncle
Benjamin, after investigation, said, "It's a blessing we
have cabins. The passengers who sleep on deck say
that everything is infested with roaches and rats."

During the three-day trip Abby ate little, making no
comment about the coarse meals with salty meats and
rancid butter. On the third evening she was relieved to

see the dock at the wooded Wayne City Landing for Independence.

Uncle Benjamin hired a buggy at the landing, and during the four-mile ride to Independence, Abby's trepidation grew. Upon arrival in the town with its shanties and log buildings, she saw it was smaller than St. Louis, but even noisier, more crowded, abustle with business. Tawdry signs lined the dirt streets: "Goods for Santa Fe trade! Goods for Oregon and California! All new and cheap!"

Seeing her consternation, Benjamin Talbot assured her, "It's much quieter where we live in the country-side."

Abby's anxieties were only somewhat alleviated. Now she wondered whether his family would be expecting them this early. Her uncle had sent a message from St. Louis about their arrival, but he had been uncertain about catching the early boat. What if his family wasn't prepared? And what if they didn't like her after all?

She must try to remember their names. There was Aunt Jessica—a widow who had run the household since Uncle Benjamin's wife, Elizabeth, had died in childbirth. Cousin Betsy, now ten years old, was the child of that birth. She would love Cousin Rena, seventeen, Daniel assured her. Jeremy, who ran the farm, was twenty and had married last fall; he and his bride, Jenny, lived in a small house on the other side of the property. Joshua, the family's trader, was now in Boston. The other two children and their families owned houses in Independence so she might not meet them until later.

It was nearly sunset when the hired buggy drove up the wooded drive to the Talbot place atop a hill. "Why, it's a log house!" Abby said with delight. They had passed frame houses and a few brick buildings, and she'd had no reason to expect such an interesting place. It was certainly not a mansion like the one in which she had grown up on Union Square, but it looked commodious.

"It's old," Uncle Benjamin said, "and we've added rooms onto rooms and wings onto wings. It's a bit of a maze, but we like the place. I suppose we shall miss it in California, but Adam and his family will be moving in so the house and land will remain in the family."

As her uncle helped her down, people hurried from the house. "Rena thought you might be home early!" the little girl who must be ten-year-old Betsy called out. "Welcome home, Papa! And, oh, welcome to our house, Cousin Abigail!"

Tears rushed to Abby's eyes as her small cousin with freckles and long auburn braids caught her in a hug.

"I'm Betsy," the girl said, her green eyes twinkling. "And this is Aunt Jessica, and here comes Reenie—I mean Rena . . . and that's Jeremy and his wife Jenny—"

"Whoa!" Benjamin Talbot laughed, "You'll have Abby's head spinning!"

"Then it's *Abby*, not Abigail?" Aunt Jessica asked as she gave her niece a warm embrace.

"Yes . . . Abby, please."

Her aunt said, "We're so happy to have you here, dear."

"It's kind of you to make me feel so welcome." The warmth in her aunt's brown eyes was as touching as her words, and she looked just as an Aunt Jessica should with her gray hair pulled back into a bun and her slight plumpness suggesting she baked pies and cookies.

Behind her aunt stood a beautiful young woman with deep dimples, hair the color of pale moonlight, and disconcerting brown eyes. "Welcome," she said, her voice as soft as the ethereal aura about her. "You do look like an Abby, not an Abigail. I've been anxious to meet you for ever so long. I know that we're going to be friends."

81

Abby did not doubt her words. "Thank you, Rena. I'm certain we shall."

Then Abby was shaking hands with Jenny, the shy dark-haired bride, and twenty-year-old Jeremy, whose hair was as auburn as little Betsy's.

At length the luggage from the buggy was carried into the old log house. Inside, a fire danced in the huge rock fireplace in the parlor, its flames imparting a warm glow to the room. Abby noticed the painting of Grandmother Talbot—so similar to that which had hung in the New York house—and flinched at the sight of the sapphire pendant.

"You're just in time for supper," Aunt Jessica said to her brother. "Your favorite—chicken fricassee."

Benjamin Talbot inquired, "And, pray tell, how were you so sure that we'd be home on an earlier boat?"

Aunt Jessica said, "We hoped so. We've missed you."

But at Abby's side little Betsy shook her head and whispered to Abby, "Rena knew. She talks to God all the time."

Abby's eyes wandered to Rena, who started lighting candles on the trestle table, her face sweet and dimpled in the candleglow. "She's very beautiful."

"Yes," Betsy agreed, "and she has lots of beaus. They all want to marry her, but she's waiting."

"Waiting?" Abby inquired.

Betsy nodded, her auburn braids bobbing against her narrow shoulders. Her green eyes went up to Abby. "I thought everybody knew."

Abby shook her head. "No, I guess that I must be the exception."

Betsy whispered, "We're not supposed to tell . . . but everyone knows that someday Rena is going to marry Daniel."

82

CHAPTER 9

A STRIDENT CROWING pierced Abby's sleep. Roosters. Yes, they often heard roosters crowing at daybreak in the village near Miss Sheffield's School. Slowly blinking awake, she glimpsed log walls and realized that she was *not* at Miss Sheffield's, not at home in New York, but in Independence, Missouri. What's more, she had spent the night sleeping in Rena's bedroom!

Immediately Betsy's words came to her: *Everyone knows that someday Rena is going to marry Daniel.*

No, it couldn't be true! Betsy was a mere child . . . what would she know?

The fragrance of lilac drifted around her, but that could only be her imagination, her confusion about being in New York. Perhaps Betsy's words were only her imagination as well.

Abby rose up on an elbow and noticed that Rena slept soundly in the other bed. This log house was not imagined, and—most likely—neither was Betsy's confidence.

Her head reeled with tortuous speculations, and it

was a long time before she could force them away to examine the room. Despite its crude log walls, the place was neat, with polished plank floors and a great round braided rug. The logs looked waxed or oiled and held frames of pressed flowers and moss. Unencumbered by her emotional turmoil, she would probably have found them pleasant decorations and this bedroom a pleasant room, different though it was from hers at home.

She slipped out of bed into the morning chill, padding to the window in her blue cotton nightgown to see if there could possibly be lilacs on the frontier.

Yes—lilacs. Just below the open window, a bush held the remnants of lavender blooms. She leaned out and reached for a dewy flower, burying her nose in its intoxicating fragrance, reminded of the lilacs at Miss Sheffield's and of those in her garden . . . at home . . . and of Cornelius that moonlit night. But the bittersweet memories must stop! She could not allow her mind to drift to the past.

The glimmering light of dawn revealed her surroundings: well-kept herb and vegetable gardens; beyond them, an orchard; in the other direction, a barn and outbuildings. One building was apparently a chicken coop since a rooster crowed from its roof as if he had raised the sun himself. To her far left was a small log cabin, undoubtedly where Jeremy and Jenny lived. It was probably more pleasant for the newlyweds to live alone, though the main house was sufficiently commodious.

At last night's dinner Aunt Jessica had explained, "I thought you might feel more comfortable sleeping with Rena tonight since the guest rooms are at the far end of the house. Tomorrow you can choose your own room."

Rena had been exceedingly kind when they had retired, but she had wanted to hear all about their journey—and unfortunately all about Daniel. If only her beautiful cousin were disagreeable in some way, it might be easier to endure this new misery. Last night Abby had examined the dilemma from every direction. To begin with, if Daniel planned to marry Rena, it explained his initial reticence to become romantically involved. Yet he *had* kissed her that night in Philadelphia; certainly he would not have done so if he planned to marry Rena. On the other hand, Cornelius had kissed her too . . . and look where that had led!

"Good morning!" Rena was sitting up in bed with a dimpled smile, clouds of pale hair falling to her pink nightgown. "What are you doing awake so early, Abby? I thought you'd be tired."

"I'm—I'm not accustomed to such wide-awake roosters," Abby responded. "And . . . then I had to see if they were truly lilacs I smelled."

Rena's lovely face dimpled more deeply. "Not only lilacs, but lilacs from *Boston!* You'll have to ask Aunt Jessica how they happen to be here in the wilds of Missouri."

"The *wilds* of Missouri!"

Rena gave a little laugh as she slipped down under her quilt again. "I only thought it must seem rustic here compared to New York. I am so happy to have you here with us! I don't want to hurt your feelings!"

"Thank you. I doubt you'd ever hurt *anyone's* feelings."

"I do try not to, Abby, but I'm not always successful."

As Abby returned to her bed and slipped in again, she was astonished to hear herself saying, "Daniel said that you are very sweet and good."

"Oh, my! That's not in the least helpful for humility!" Rena laughingly protested. "How did he happen to say that?"

"He told me a bit about everyone in the family. He was probably trying to make it easier for me to become acquainted."

"What else did he say about us?"

"That you were all more educated than the usual frontier family, thanks to Harvard, the University of Missouri, and Aunt Jessica . . . and that you'd welcome me with open arms, as you did him."

Rena smiled. "Daniel is easy to love."

Abby's spirits sank. "Yes."

"Now that you're certain we have lilacs in Missouri, you must try to sleep again," Rena suggested sweetly. "You've had such a long trip."

"Yes, maybe I should."

She pulled the warm covers up behind her neck, wishing that the entire family were not quite so laudable. Last night when they had settled at the supper table, she had expected them to say grace before the meal. Instead, everyone had held hands, both Aunt Jessica and Betsy smiling as they took her hands. Then they had all sung quite fervently:

Praise God, from whom all blessings flow;
Praise Him, all creatures here below;
Praise Him above, ye heavenly host;
Praise Father, Son, and Holy Ghost.

They had ended with a harmonious amen, her own voice absent from the beautiful prayer. No one had mentioned her failure to join in, so perhaps they hadn't noticed. *This is how Daniel was raised!*

She snuggled deeper under the covers and decided that she would have to make a great effort to fit into this family, to fit into his kind of life. Anxious over what the morning would bring, what the entire day might bring, she finally drifted off to an uneasy sleep.

At breakfast she was prepared to join hands for prayer and to sing, but this morning they sang a different prayer:

O, for a thousand tongues to sing
My great Redeemer's praise,
The glories of my God and King,
The triumphs of His grace!

Their eyes were closed and Abby glanced around the table at them: Uncle Benjamin in his black broadcloth suit, Aunt Jessica in a serviceable black dress and white mobcap over her gray hair, Rena in a rose frock that enhanced her pale beauty, and Betsy in a green dress to match her eyes. The plump hired girl, Sarah, had returned to the kitchen. All sang with vigor, joyful smiles lighting their faces as they started the next verse.

My gracious Master and my God,
Assist me to proclaim,
To spread thro' all the earth abroad
The honors of Thy name.

While they sang their amen, Abby supposed that it was not so unusual that the offspring of a clergyman would sing grace at meals. It was probably more surprising to them that she—that same clergyman's granddaughter—did not even *know* the words. She glanced around the table, but the others were now occupied with passing the food. She would learn, she vowed again; she would learn all of it to please Daniel.

After they had passed the platters of bacon, eggs, and biscuits around the table, Rena said, "Abby could hardly believe that we had lilacs here in Missouri, Aunt Jessica. You'll have to tell her how they happen to be here."

"Yes, I would like to know," Abby said, stirring cream into her steaming coffee.

Aunt Jessica spread honey on a biscuit. "You know that I was born in Boston. Well, after I married Noah we moved to a farm in Pennsylvania, and my mother—Grandmother Talbot—gave me roots from the lilacs and my favorite red rosebush.

"Well, Noah was restless, and after some years he felt that there were too many people in Pennsylvania. So we moved to Ohio by covered wagon, taking along the roots of the lilacs and the rosebush, not to mention all of our other belongings. It was wild country, all woods and Indians. But more settlers came, and Noah wanted to move again. We went to Kentucky in an oxcart pulled by four oxen. Sometimes the trail was so narrow that Noah had to chop down trees to get the cart through.''

Abby prompted, "And you took your lilac and rose roots?"

Her aunt sighed. "Indeed I did. I was glad to have them. It was lonely living so close to the forest, especially at night. Wolves howled, and once a bear stole our bacon. Noah overcame his restlessness when he found the Lord, and we stayed there until Noah passed on to be with Him." For a moment she stared into the distance. "Then I traveled here with my lilac and rosebush roots when Benjamin invited me. It seems to me now that the beauty and perfume of their flowers help us sense the Lord's presence. I'm glad I brought them."

Uncle Benjamin said, "You brought me and *seven* children a heart full of patience and love. You've been a wonderful aunt to them."

"Now you mustn't flatter me, Benjamin! I'd been praying all my life for children, and suddenly my prayers were answered. Seven children! If Daniel were here," Aunt Jessica protested, "he would help me by quoting a verse on the evils of flattery!"

"Probably three or four verses!" Rena added, to everyone's amusement.

How much better all of them know him than I do! Abby realized.

Betsy said, "We mustn't forget to take the roots along to California next spring."

Aunt Jessica smiled. "It seems that most of my life has been devoted to carrying those roots around this country. Wouldn't it be like me to forget the roots for my last move?"

Benjamin Talbot's brown eyes twinkled. "And what makes you think that traveling to California is your last move?"

His sister said with a flash of humor, "Because I'm not going to have to dig them up and carry them along to glory!"

Benjamin laughed. "No, that's one place where we won't have to bring anything except our love for the Lord. Wouldn't it be easy to move if that's all we had to carry along!"

Abby felt as uncomfortable when they mentioned next spring's trip to California as she did about their religious remarks. They brought religion into everything, and it made her feel like an outsider.

After breakfast Aunt Jessica showed Abby the guest rooms. "I thought you might like this one with the river view," she suggested. "It's larger and has north light for painting."

Abby glanced out the window. Just below the property was a dirt road where covered wagons had lined up to leave for the West. She could scarcely endure the scene—the reminder that next spring she would have to move again. Yet she sensed she would sketch this picture, this westward march of pioneers as surely as she was watching those below now. While she and Aunt Jessica stood before the window, the oxen and wagons stirred to a start with a great racket of shouts and whips; it seemed an entire pastureful of cattle was to follow in the dust. "It looks awful, Aunt Jessica. Why do they go?"

"For many reasons, I suppose. Some for cheap land, more than a few to escape the law, others to get away from the fevers that kill entire families. Three little Talbot children died of fever right in this house."

Abby did not care to hear of dying. "There must be other reasons people go West."

"Some are just plain restless living on farms, and they desperately want to embark on one great adventure in their lives. After all, a good many of their parents moved west at one time or another, even if it was just a distance of one or two states. They heard

89

their parents' or grandparents' stories about when they 'moved out west' so often that it seems right to them to go. When I taught school in Pennsylvania, Ohio, and Kentucky, that's what I heard . . . 'wun Grandpappy moved west,' or 'wun Pappy moved to Kentuck,' or 'I hain't stayin' here, I be movin' west too wun I'm growed up.' "

Abby smiled at her aunt's imitation of the vernacular that had become increasingly prevalent on the trip to Missouri.

Aunt Jessica added, "Sometimes I think our emigrating to California is no different, though Benjamin and the boys insist it's to expand their trade."

"What about manifest destiny? It's been in newspapers and on everyone's lips all through our journey here."

Her aunt gazed out at the departing pioneers. "Yes, the westward movement is becoming a crusade—a manifest destiny that we overspread the continent with the blessings of liberty and democracy. I tend to agree, but particularly that we must overspread the earth with God's love. It is, after all, the Great Commission."

Abby was not certain she understood; so much about Christianity seemed unclear to her.

Later in the morning, Betsy was pleased to show her around the small farm and around the barn and other outbuildings.

Near the well house was a jouncing seat that her uncle had built for the children, and, in a shed with the sleigh, homemade sleds for each child. How different Uncle Benjamin was from her own father, Abby thought. Her father would never have built anything for anyone, though he had been generous with money . . . generous to a fault!

After lunch Abby arranged her belongings in her log-walled bedroom, setting up the collapsible easel Daniel had given her; she carefully placed on it her sketch of him asleep on the train. Just looking at the picture made her heart overflow with love.

That evening after supper, Uncle Benjamin suggested that Abby share her watercolor sketches of the trip with the family, and Betsy helped fetch them from Abby's bedroom. "Aren't we taking the one of Daniel?" she asked, her green eyes brimming with interest. "I like it best."

Abby flushed. "It—it's not quite finished yet." She quickly removed it from the easel and placed it upon her bureau. If any of the others saw the sketch they might deduce that she loved him!

In the parlor, Rena was particularly enthusiastic about Abby's work. "I've always wondered what New York and Pittsburgh and Cincinnati and Louisville looked like—and here they are! It's wonderful, Abby. God has given you a great gift!"

A gift? Abby blinked, though her art teachers had called her gifted. "Yes, I–I guess so."

Aunt Jessica added, "They are very good, Abby. Do you think you could do a sketch of your grandmother, our first Abigail Talbot? Of all the things we must leave behind when we move to California, I think that I'll miss that portrait of Mother the most. We're afraid to risk it on the trip."

Abby looked up at the familiar oil painting of her grandmother, so similar to the one she'd known in New York. Grandmother Talbot wore her golden hair in a chignon, a cerulean-blue gown emphasizing the glow in her sapphire eyes—and the pendant that Abby had sold. "I don't know. I–I've never sketched from a portrait."

"I hope you'll try," Uncle Benjamin urged. "It would be a great favor to us if we could take a likeness of Mother along. There were no daguerreotypes in her day, of course, and we only have this portrait, which we're leaving with Adam and his family."

"I'll try." Their confidence overwhelmed her.

On Sunday morning they brought a vase of wild red roses to the small white church with its simple steeple, and Aunt Jessica reverently arranged them on the altar before other members of the congregation arrived. Abby sat down in the oak pew between her uncle and Rena, reminded of the elegant New York church where she had attended with Uncle Benjamin and Daniel. In this church, however, there were no stained-glass windows, no Gothic towers, no magnificent organ . . . and no Daniel. Here she sat next to Rena, who wore a lavender dress she had made with her own delicate hands; she was surely the most beautiful young woman in Missouri—and she was expecting to marry Daniel!

CHAPTER 10

ABBY BOWED HER HEAD, her thoughts so scattered that she was unable to say anything to God. If He did exist, she assuredly should not ask for Him to take away Daniel from Rena. That would be selfish. Finally the service began with the small organ wheezing out an anthem, and Abby rose with the small congregation. Rena shared her hymnal, singing out exquisitely with the others in her melodious contralto:

Praise to the Lord, ye heavens, adore him;
Praise him, angels, in the height;
Sun and moon, rejoice before him;
Praise him, all ye stars of light.
Praise the Lord: for he hath spoken;
Words his mighty voice obeyed;
Law which never shall be broken
For their guidance hath he made.

Rena's "gift" was clear. As if she were not beautiful and sweet enough, she sang like an angel! Abby mouthed the words, knowing she would hit a false note if she even attempted to sing.

The young brown-haired minister, Reverend Seth

Thompson, was rather handsome in his black broad-cloth suit. His sermon dealt with forgiveness, reminding Abby of the lecture Daniel had given her about forgiving her parents and Roxanna Murray . . . and Cornelius. She had, after all, led him on so she couldn't blame him entirely for his ungentlemanly expectations. Moreover, she must write to thank his parents for the reception and to let his mother know she had arrived safely in Independence.

Reverend Thompson quoted from Ephesians 4:32: "And be ye kind one to another, tenderhearted, forgiving one another, even as God for Christ's sake hath forgiven you."

Oddly enough, Abby suddenly felt tenderhearted toward Cornelius and she thought, *Yes, I do forgive him.*

After church, she was introduced to Reverend Thompson, who was kind, but clearly had a special interest in Rena. Nor was he the only man intrigued by Rena's pale beauty and disconcerting brown eyes. It seemed that every young man in the church stopped by to exchange a hopeful word with Rena Talbot. Rena, in turn, introduced them to Abby, who in her black crepe dress felt as plain as a wren beside an exotic bird. She must have conveyed her self-consciousness for the young men almost immediately turned back to Rena.

Later Reverend Thompson joined them at the Talbot house for a pleasant dinner, after which he and Rena departed for an afternoon stroll.

Abby hopefully asked Aunt Jessica, "Is Rena in love with the minister?"

Her aunt appeared taken aback. "Why, not to my knowledge. Seth is a Christian brother to her. I think he simply wants her suggestions for church music and social events."

Behind them Betsy pronounced, "Even Reverend Thompson knows that Rena is going to marry Daniel."

Aunt Jessica said firmly, "Now, Betsy, you mustn't meddle," and Abby left the room as soon as it seemed suitable.

As the days passed, Abby felt more and more at home, toiling with Betsy in the herb and vegetable gardens every morning. She began to feel a pleasure in working the warm crumbly soil with her hands, in the sprouting seeds, and in the sun warming her back as she weeded and hoed. This was her time of healing, of drawing beauty from the flowers and joy from the singing of the birds. One balmy morning when Rena brought out cold buttermilk to them, Abby mentioned her pleasure in the garden, particularly the flowers.

Rena smiled. "I think we should consider ourselves to be flowers that God created to give off His fragrance of love to others on earth."

How often her cousin spoke like that, Abby thought, yet she was not falsely pious. Rena brimmed with love and laughter and an inner joy. At first Abby resented Rena's failure to garden; instead, her cousin mended, sewed, set the table, and did other quiet work. One day Aunt Jessica explained, "Rena is not as strong as the rest of us. Her health is delicate, but we must not seem too aware of it. She likes to do her part."

Abby began to notice that whenever Rena thought herself alone she looked frail, but with others, love transformed her so thoroughly that she seemed strong and enthusiastic, and when she sang solos in church, her melodious contralto voice filled with such power that she seemed to soar.

On another morning when Rena again carried cold buttermilk out to the garden, Abby suddenly said, "Oh, Rena, I wish that you weren't always so good."

"But I am not good at all!" Rena protested. "I am just like the apostle Paul when he said, 'For the good that I would I do not: but the evil which I would not, that I do.'"

"*You* do evil?" Abby protested.

"Oh, yes. I am forever asking His forgiveness."

"But whatever for?"

Rena's eyes filled with dismay. "I forget to look for the good in others and to love the good in them. I forget to see my unworthiness compared with everyone's worth. And I forget to hush my heart and bid all of my senses be still so that I might have perfect communion with the Lord. I become too full of *self*."

Another day Rena said, "I think we must love and laugh more, to make the world around us happy. I think our love and joy are like the ripples when we throw a stone in a pond, spreading out in ever-widening circles, far beyond our knowledge, and such love and joy are eternal."

It struck Abby as unrealistic. She recalled her father's dabbling in the New England philosophy that said man could achieve perfection. "Can you make yourself perfect?"

"Never!" Rena protested. "Only the Lord, Jesus Christ, is perfect!"

"Is?" Abby asked.

"Yes! He was and is and always will be!"

"I daresay I don't understand."

Rena's eyes glowed. "He came to earth so that we might know God through Him."

"You mean that Christ is the bridge . . . the way to God?"

"Yes! And the way to live forever with love and joy!"

If Abby did not quite understand Rena, she did understand Betsy, who told her everything she knew about herbs, vegetables, and the town of Independence . . . but nothing more about Daniel.

August 1, 1845

My dear friend, Rose,

96

I have been hoping to hear from you, but you must be busy with your married life. Forgive me for not having sent a wedding gift. There is nothing suitable here unless you would like a buffalo robe, moccasins, or provisions for a covered wagon trip to the far West. I am exaggerating slightly, but this is not New York!

Independence is a raucous frontier town with log-cabin and shanty saddlers' shops, smithies, saloons, carpenter shops, and frontier trading posts lining the dirt street. (Uncle Benjamin and his sons own the largest and most pleasant of the trading posts.) At first I was so appalled at the town that I could not bear it, but now I find it more interesting and have sketched it.

Fortunately we live in a large, comfortable log house in the countryside, and my relations have been wonderfully kind to me. I am slowly growing accustomed to the frontier. Now, in August, it is more bearable since no settlers are moving west in this awful heat, but there are still Indians and drunken river roustabouts.

Much to my surprise, everyone admires my watercolor sketches, and I have even sold some through my uncle's trading post—no doubt because there is so little else to give as gifts! It occurred to me that I could send several pictures as a wedding gift for you and William. I hope my gift will not be too rustic. I visualize you and William amid crystal chandeliers and fine French antiques, but perhaps the pictures will be suitable for your library as studies of the West.

This great undertaking of sending a wedding gift will occur when Cousin Joshua arrives, then departs for Washington in the next few weeks. Daniel is coming with him! It seems years ago, not mere months, that I saw him and my ardor has not diminished. But, oh, Rose, it appears we are star-crossed lovers for everyone expects him to marry my cousin, Rena! I waver between heartache and hope. I had no idea that love could be so wonderful and at the same time a wrenching torment. I scarcely know how I will react when Daniel arrives. When he is near, Miss Sheffield's admonitions for moderation take flight.

I did have an opportunity to wear your precious Fleur-de-lis *last week as the schoolmaster, Horace Litmer, took*

me out walking after church and Sunday dinner. He is
about thirty years old and pleasant, but I do not love him.
Moreover, I'm sure that he loves Cousin Rena. Every
man in Independence seems to and one cannot blame
them for she must be the most beautiful (and dear) young
lady hereabouts.

How happy I am for you—married now to your dear
William. Please convey my best wishes to him.

> *Affectionately,*
> *Abby*

P.S. I have had a contrite *letter from Cornelius! His*
grandmother, it seems, is in failing health. He may visit
Missouri on business for the bank someday!

It was no accident that Abby and Betsy were
sketching under a cottonwood tree near the water-
front when the *Liberty* steamed in from St. Louis.
Since Betsy appeared to have an artistic bent, they
had been sketching scenes all over Independence,
albeit near the wharf every afternoon this week. Aunt
Jessica did not entirely approve of their proximity to
dock roustabouts and gave in only because shipping
activity had quieted for summer. In addition, she
insisted that old Moses, a free black worker at
Talbot's Trading Post, drive them out in the buggy
and stay with them.

"Do you think that's their boat?" Betsy asked over
the sound of the rushing river.

"I don't know," Abby replied as calmly as possible
as the *Liberty* steamed to the dock. She did have a
feeling about the boat, but she had been having
"feelings" about every Missouri boat that had docked
for the past week.

"Sketch it into your picture, Betsy," she suggested. "A boat coming in always lends a sense of
expectancy." She penciled in the sturdy sternwheeler
with its snub-nosed prow and twin smokestacks like
rabbit's ears, and her own expectancy colored the
scene with excitement. *Daniel's Arrival* she entitled it
hopefully.

"There they are on the deck!" Betsy exclaimed. "It's Daniel and Joshua!"

Abby squinted against the sunshine to the distant boat, disbelieving because she so fervently wished it to be true. "Are you sure?" One of the men in Eastern dress did remind her of Daniel—his height, towering over most of the other passengers near the gangplank, his broad shoulders, even his manner and firm stance.

"I'm certain! Come on, let's get Moses to drive the buggy over for them!" Betsy grabbed her sketching supplies and raced toward the buggy, where Moses and the horses drowsed under cottonwood trees in the afternoon heat.

In a daze, Abby attempted to organize her papers and pencils, her eyes scarcely leaving the man who resembled Daniel. To her astonishment, he waved.

Abby's heart knocked against her ribs so loudly that she was certain Betsy and Moses could hear. "It appears that Daniel and Joshua have arrived," she told the old man.

"So I hear, Miz Abby," he said, brushing the dust from his clothes before helping her up into the buggy.

"Please hurry!" she urged Moses.

"Yez'um." He cocked a curious brow at her before ambling around and climbing up onto his seat.

It seemed forever before the horses traversed the short distance on the rutted road, raising dust at the edge of the dock. Daniel and his companion were already walking down the gangplank.

"Abby! Betsy!" Daniel called out with a great smile.

Abby was out of the buggy before Moses could help her down, and she might have run straight into Daniel's arms if an inexplicable shyness hadn't overtaken her at the last instant. "Daniel . . ."

His blue eyes caught her in their steady gaze, then quite suddenly her hand was in his and he was kissing her fingertips again. "You're looking fine now, Abby," he said with a peculiar roughness in his voice.

Behind them Joshua had already hugged Betsy and now he commented dryly, "Aren't you going to introduce me to my cousin, Daniel?"

Daniel's color rose and before he could begin the introduction, Betsy excitedly put in, "Abby, this is my brother, Joshua!"

Joshua nodded slightly. "It is a pleasure to meet you, Abby. Now I see why Daniel wanted to stop in Independence."

Abby fought the blush rising to her cheeks. "I have been looking forward to meeting you," she mustered, barely recovering her wits. This second son of Benjamin Talbot resembled his father only in the square chin and brown eyes. A toughness in the set of his chin, a daring in his eyes, told Abby he was no doubt a firm trader for the family's business, and he was quite handsome, with a dashing mustache, and dark auburn hair.

Betsy said into the silence, "Abby's been teaching me to draw. We've been drawing the wharf all this week."

"I see." Daniel glanced at Abby quizzically.

She managed an innocent smile, and they started toward Moses and the buggy.

Only a few minutes were required for the men to help Moses strap their baggage onto the back of the buggy. Then Daniel helped Abby into the back seat, his nearness unnerving her so that she almost missed the step. He sat down beside her, and Betsy and Joshua sat on the driver's seat with Moses.

As they rode away from the wharf toward Independence, Abby silently and nervously smoothed her black dress, wishing that she were no longer in mourning.

"I am delighted to see that you are still sketching," Daniel said as they jounced along the rutted road.

"Yes, thanks to your gift of the portable case."

"That was my pleasure. Aunt Jessica wrote that some of your pictures have even been sold at the trading post."

"Yes, five watercolor sketches. But I made copies so you could see the entire trip as if you were with us."

His smile was a brilliant white in the sunshine. "I knew you had talent when I first saw your sketches of the garden and house in New York. You have that rare knack of capturing the spirit of a place. And I knew you had perseverance when you forced yourself to work despite your troubles."

Joshua called over his shoulder, his toughness replaced with a trace of amusement. "Sounds mighty serious back there. Just what sort of verse are you already quoting to my pretty cousin?"

Daniel chuckled. "I was circling the topic of perseverance."

"I can imagine," Joshua replied dubiously.

As if to prove himself Daniel quoted, "An enterprise, when fairly once begun, should not be left till all that ought is won." Oddly enough, he directed the words to her.

"Shakespeare, I presume," Joshua said, "but I'll catch you without a quote on something yet."

Abby's mind darted to the enterprise of that night in Philadelphia when he had kissed her. Had that been the enterprise he recalled with that gleam in his eyes? Blushing, she asked, "How is it that you can remember so many quotations, Daniel?"

He smiled. "It's very simple. You have a gift for art, and I have a gift for memory."

"My eye!" Joshua put in. "Instead of sleeping nights like most people, old Daniel stays awake, memorizing those blamed quotations so he can flay us with them all day!"

"Exactly!" Daniel agreed with a laugh. "Moreover, you've given us a fine example of perseverance!"

Even Moses chuckled as he flicked the reins lightly over the horses. "Home, boys," he said. "Home."

If only they didn't have to go home, Abby thought with a rush of trepidation. She could happily ride along in this buggy with Daniel at her side forever.

At length they turned into the drive lined with black walnut trees and oaks. "Well, here we are!" Daniel announced.

The buggy stopped at the door of the Talbots' log house, where Rena and Aunt Jessica sat shelling peas for dinner.

Rena rose, unaware that the pan of peas spilled at her feet. Such a flash of joy crossed her dimpled face that Abby knew she would remember it forever. She stood beside Daniel while her cousin rushed to his arms.

"Oh, Daniel!" Rena cried out against his shoulder, "you're home! At long last, you're home!"

Tears flooded Abby's eyes. Betsy's words that first night were true. *Everyone knows that someday Rena is going to marry Daniel.*

CHAPTER 11

BEFORE MOSES DEPARTED for town with the buggy, Aunt Jessica asked him to carry news of Daniel's and Joshua's arrival and to invite the rest of the family for supper. That evening, when the entire clan congregated, Abby was easily able to separate the in-laws from the Talbots, who, with the exception of Rena, were auburn-haired.

She watched the brothers and sisters arrive with baskets of food as she set the expanded dining room table. They embraced Daniel and Joshua. "About time you came home!" they said, and, "When are you two going to settle down?"

Daniel and Joshua laughed off their questions.

"Here's what happens if you do," Adam said, proudly showing off his wife, Inga, and their five children ranging in age from one to six. At thirty Adam was the eldest, the family's gentle giant; he had attended Harvard with Daniel and Joshua, and, according to Daniel, spent his time there pining for Inga, whom he had promptly married upon his return to Independence. Adam's hair was reddest, but his eyes were a contented brown. He and Inga would move here, into the home place with their brood when the others left for California.

Martha Talbot Baker, whose two small sons hid behind her skirt, teased, "Or you could have twins like me!"

Luke, her husband, grinned. "Now, Martha, you're going to scare 'em. Besides, twins run in my family, not the Talbots."

Benjamin Talbot announced, "And here come the newlyweds!"

Jeremy and Jenny smiled shyly, carrying warm peach pies that smelled ambrosial.

At length the women excused themselves to take their dishes to the kitchen. Abby was still setting the table when Rena arrived in the parlor to serve cold buttermilk to the men. Silverware in hand, Abby quailed at the adoring gaze Daniel bestowed upon her cousin. It was true that even Rena's brothers adored her and that she had embraced Joshua with equal enthusiasm upon their arrival—but Daniel was *not* her brother!

Quickly completing the table settings, Abby hurried through the hustle of the women in the kitchen to set the children's table. After a while she offered, "Perhaps I can sit in the kitchen to help the children, Aunt Jessica. Then all of your family can be together . . . all of the grown-ups."

Inga said with her slight German accent, "I sit at the children's table. I am used to five children, and the twins have already eaten."

"I could help," Abby offered.

Aunt Jessica said, "Well, then, if you like. It will give the two of you a chance to become better acquainted."

Abby breathed a sigh of relief at not having to watch Daniel and Rena gaze at each other. She returned to the dining room to remove a place setting,

104

and saw them laughing about something together. She quickly finished her task and fled.

Adam and Inga, and Martha and Luke left shortly after supper with their children. Since Sarah, the hired girl, was cleaning up, there was nothing for Abby to do but join the others in the parlor.

"Ah, there you are, Abby!" Daniel rose from the horsehair sofa where he had been chatting with Betsy. "I've been looking forward to seeing your pictures."

"Then if you'll excuse me, I'll get them," Abby said with a blush and started for her room.

Betsy joined her in the hallway. "Can I help carry them?"

Abby gave one of her small cousin's red braids a playful tug. "*May* I?" she corrected gently.

"*May* I help carry them?"

"Yes, you may," Abby replied with a smile.

In her room she quickly assembled the watercolors of her trip west, including the four framed for Rose's wedding gift.

"Aren't you going to take the one of Daniel sleeping in the train?" Betsy asked. "I like it best."

Abby faltered. "N–no, I don't think so. He's already seen it."

"But Joshua hasn't."

"I'm sure that Joshua has seen enough of Daniel sleeping since they've been traveling together," Abby said, unwilling to share the sketch. She handed several of the pictures to Betsy. "This should be enough for tonight."

In the parlor, Daniel moved to the middle of the sofa to make room for her and Betsy on either side.

Abby settled down with trepidation, warmed at his nearness.

"I have the pictures of when you left New York," Betsy said. "Shall I start?"

"Fine," Abby replied, welcoming time to quiet the hammering of her heart.

"This is the first," Betsy explained. "Abby numbered them."

She watched Daniel study the river scene. It was no longer the black and white picture she had sketched upon their departure at the North River; she had painted in the blues of the sky and the river, the whites, silvers, and tans of boats, and the bright dashes of yellows, reds, and greens of the passengers' and roustabouts' clothing. "It's very good," he said. "I can understand why people are buying them."

"Thank you," Abby replied, realizing how important his approval was to her.

"Look at this," Betsy urged, and he continued through the pictures, marveling at how well the scenes had been captured, passing them on to Joshua, who was equally impressed.

While Daniel studied the pictures, Abby noted the short curly hairs on the backs of his hands and his fingers, as dark as his hair and beard; his hands were broad with long fingers, his fingernails clean and neatly cut. How she would like to touch his hands.

After he viewed the pictures Betsy held, Daniel turned to Abby's. She passed him the first sketch of the Mississippi River with its colorful jumble of boats, and their fingers touched. For an instant it felt as though lightning had struck her hand, and she caught her breath at the jolt of astonishment in his blue eyes as they looked into hers.

At length he returned to the pictures and said somewhat breathlessly, "It's very good, Abby. They're all very good."

She slowly let out her own breath before she could say, "Thank you, Daniel." Everyone in the parlor must be aware of their attraction, she thought, yet when she dared look, it appeared that no one had noticed except perhaps Betsy, whose green eyes were filled with bewilderment.

The next day was Saturday, and Daniel and Joshua

accompanied Benjamin Talbot to the trading post to make arrangements for future shipments of merchandise. That evening after supper, the family took up the matter of their wagon train trek to California.

Benjamin Talbot said, "Now that the way to California is established, I think the number of wagon trains will increase. Five thousand people set out for Oregon or California last year. We'll have to beat the crowd so there's ample grass for the oxen near the trail. I'd suggest we depart in early May, no matter how high the rivers are here."

As soon as it was expedient, Abby excused herself. The idea of traveling by covered wagon through prairies, deserts, and over two chains of mountains was sufficiently daunting, and hearing the hardships of other travelers did not help. And then having to endure Rena and Daniel's togetherness!

When she slipped into bed and tried to calm her mind for the night, she half-prayed, "If You are out there somewhere, God, I don't want to go! Please, I don't want to go!"

Before church on Sunday morning, Daniel said to Abby as they stepped out the door, "What are you so concerned about?"

Am I that transparent? she wondered. She hoped he didn't realize how disinclined she was to move to California . . . or that she was jealous . . . yes, jealous of Rena. Worse, Rena would sing a solo at church this morning.

Abby temporized, "I have to ask Joshua to deliver the four framed pictures to my friend Rose back East. She was my roommate at Miss Sheffield's. They're a wedding gift."

"And a fine one," Daniel said, his hand at her elbow to help her down the steps. "I'll discuss it with Joshua for you. Sometimes he enjoys being difficult."

"Thank you." She smiled up at Daniel. He wore his black broadcloth suit and looked terribly handsome.

He glanced about to make certain they were alone. "We'll have to bank the remainder of your money tomorrow morning."

Panic rose to Abby's throat. "What will Uncle Benjamin say about the pendant money? As it was, I had a difficult time forcing him to accept payment for the trip here."

"I see no reason for you to explain. After all, the pendant belonged to you. I'll borrow Jeremy's buggy, and we'll wait until your uncle and Joshua have left for work. If they ask, I'll tell them I have private business to attend to." He added thoughtfully, "You do like to pay your own way, don't you, Abby?"

"Yes. Yes, I do."

His forehead furrowed slightly. "You'll find someday that it's not always possible."

"I'm afraid I don't understand—" she began.

The rest of the family joined them in the shade while Joshua and Jeremy brought around the buggies. Rena's pale hair was swept into a French braid, and she wore a lovely azure frock. She dimpled with joy when Abby and Daniel greeted her.

Uncle Benjamin said to Daniel, "It will be good to have you and Joshua in the family pew again."

"It will be good to be there," Daniel replied.

Later, in the back seat of the buggy as they approached the small white frame church, Daniel asked her in a serious tone, "Do you know the Lord, Abby?"

His question struck her as peculiar since, after all, she was going to church with him. "I've gone to church every Sunday since I've lived here."

Instead of appearing gratified, Daniel simply responded, "I see."

Abby bristled. After all, she had been attending mainly to please him.

Inside the church, she sat between Daniel and Joshua. She watched Daniel from the corner of her

eye as the service progressed, although after a while
she decided it was unnecessary to be circumspect. His
attention was so centered upon the service that he
seemed unaware of her. She marveled at his obvious
faith and the joyous dignity in his low voice as he sang
out with the congregation:

When morning gilds the skies, my heart awaking cries,
May Jesus Christ be praised! . . .

Joshua, she noted, sang with considerably less
fervency.

After the Bible study, announcements, and morning
prayer, it was time for Rena's solo, and she stepped
quietly from the front pew to the altar, waiting while
the organist played the introduction. Standing there in
her blue dress, Rena gazed upward toward the back of
her church, and her enthralling contralto voice filled
the church like a loving presence:

Amazing grace! how sweet the sound,
That saved a wretch like me!
I once was lost, but now am found
Was blind, but now I see.

Did Rena think herself a wretch? Abby wondered as
the lovely voice soared. She was one of the finest
people Abby had ever known!

Abby glanced around and noticed that several
women dabbed at their eyes; as for Daniel, the
expression on his face betrayed how deeply he was
touched. It seemed to Abby that either she was
insensitive or that she still remained on the outer
edges of a mystery.

The church picnic that afternoon was a great
success, and Abby was never again alone with Daniel
until Monday morning. Fortuitously no one else was
about when they set out in the buggy for the bank.

"I appreciate your keeping my secret about selling
the pendant," she said.

He nodded. Most likely he didn't approve of selling
it, though he had never said so.

Despite the stifling August mugginess, she wore her best black cotton dress for the short ride into town, trying to overcome the foreboding that rose in her like the distant dark clouds. It appeared that another Missouri storm loomed.

"Joshua and I will be leaving tomorrow morning," Daniel remarked off-handedly.

"So soon?" She attempted to hide her disappointment. "I thought you might stay a week."

He kept his eyes on the horses as they trotted into town. "I have numerous affairs to conclude back East before the move to California."

She blurted, "I'm going to—miss you, Daniel."

He frowned, and beneath his beard it was apparent that his jawline hardened. "I'm going to miss you too." He pulled on the reins, directing their team through the horses and wagons and buggies on Independence's main street.

After a lengthy silence, he turned to her. "Abby?"

"Yes?"

"Nothing," he said, "nothing."

What was this *nothing* that he had nearly said? If only he were not so circumspect!

He helped her out of the buggy, and she was heartened to see the tenderness on his face. He did care for her, she thought, with a flood of happiness. He did care for her! Walking to the bank, the noisy town no longer seemed so ramshackle or raucous; even the deafening racket at the wagonwrights and the clamor of hammers pounding hot iron at the smithies receded. With Daniel at her side she paid no heed to the dark clouds scudding across the sky toward Independence.

Later, when their business at the bank was concluded, they stepped outside. The wind sent billowing clouds of dust through the town. Horses at the hitching posts whinnied, and the hoofs of other horses clopped against the dirt road as people hastily headed their horses, wagons, and buggies home.

"We're in for a fast storm," Daniel said, shielding his eyes against the airborne grit.

Abby clutched her flapping skirt. "Maybe it'll blow over." Storms here often did, though today the sky was darkly ominous.

He took her arm, and they struggled against the wind toward the horses and buggy.

With Daniel's assistance, Abby climbed up into the buggy, her skirt and petticoats flying. She was grateful for Daniel's strong arm around her shoulders, for the pleasure of his touch and the strength of his presence. Thunder rumbled across the sky as they hurriedly settled themselves in the buggy.

Daniel took up the reins and flicked them against the horses. "Home, boys!" he shouted into the wind.

Driving through the whirling grit, they dodged farm wagons and buggies, their occupants intent on beating the storm home. Black clouds obscured the entire sky now, rushing toward them. High above, lightning cracked.

"Hang on!" Daniel warned, "We'll soon be home."

Abby clung to the buggy seat as they raced out of town with the wind. A light drizzle fell, then a driving rain, and, suddenly a downpour that soaked them to the skin. Daniel drove the horses past the Talbot house and directly to the barn. "I'll open the doors!" he shouted. "Can you drive them in?"

"Yes!" She took the reins and he jumped down, running through the downpour for the barn doors and pulling them open. She drove the horses in, and Daniel grabbed them by the harness.

Finally he was helping her down from the buggy. "You look like a drenched cat," he said with a grin.

"So do you!" she returned. "No, with that beard, more like a drenched bear!" Suddenly her foot slipped on the wet buggy step. "Oh!" She grabbed for a handhold, but too late, and fell.

Daniel caught her and staggered back, regaining his balance and holding her wet body against his. His eyes met hers in astonishment, and he slowly and silently let her down until her feet touched the barn's dirt floor. At length his arms loosened their grip around her back.

Outside, rain pelted the earth, and, inside, the smells of the storm and damp straw and . . . the masculine smell of Daniel . . . flooded her senses. His shoulders and chest were hard under his soaked clothing; his breath was hot in her hair. Now was the time to back away, she firmly told herself, but her senses were fired, aflame for his kiss. Instead of moving away, her hands slipped around his muscular back, and she gazed up hopelessly at him.

"Abby . . ."

She tilted her mouth up to his, and his lips met hers with hesitation, then with such mounting passion that she was lost, consumed and engulfed by desire. *Love me, Daniel!* her entire being begged. *Please love me!*

He kissed her again and again, holding her ever closer until she was certain that he did love her as much as she loved him. He had once spoken of a love that was like stealing fire from heaven—and now they had discovered it.

An eternity seemed to pass before they moved away to catch their breath. The rain had stopped, though the rolls of thunder boomed through the sky as if from a celestial drum. Outside the open barn doors, the earth steamed. It was a long moment before she realized that only a sprawling oak tree shielded them from the view of anyone in the house. As she peered over his shoulder, thunder reverberated again and a flash of lightning zigzagged down from the sky, splitting the oak tree. She stared at its charred and smoking trunk.

"No," Daniel said, his face a study in stern denial as he moved away from her. "No, Abby. No more."

"But I love you, Daniel!"

He closed his eyes in pain. "You must never say that to a man, Abby." His tone was rigid with determination.

Was it wrong to feel so in love? she wondered, backing away from him. A flash of remembrance hit. It was because of Rena . . . always Rena.

Tears clouded Abby's eyes, and she and Daniel stood as far apart as strangers at the barn door while they watched the storm move on, its dark clouds billowing and lit by occasional lightning flashes.

Daniel turned away, his voice harsh and regretful. "I have to unharness the horses."

Abby choked at his coldness and tore herself from his presence, running wildly through the wet grass, as terrified by her own passion as she was confused by Daniel's vacillation. Inside the house, she ran to her room.

She felt too unwell to join the family for dinner, and Daniel was not there for supper.

He departed at dawn, disappearing like the storm that had ignited their passions, leaving only the split oak tree, its branches charred.

CHAPTER 12

THE STORMS OF SUMMER ENDED and yielded to the fiery foliage of autumn. Fields of goldenrod colored the rolling countryside; sumacs blazed brilliant scarlets; maples, with yellows, oranges, and reds; sprawling oaks, with yellows and browns. Even the split oak near the barn lived on.

Betsy returned to school, and Abby taught drawing to the two young daughters of one of the prosperous traders, spending her small income on painting supplies and birthday gifts. At home, they finished drying the last of the fall apples, adding them to their store of dried peaches, pears, and summer apples for the trip to California. Horace Litmer, the lantern-jawed, green-eyed schoolmaster, sometimes called upon Abby, but his eyes always drifted toward Rena, who discouraged all beaus now as if she were waiting for Daniel.

Cornelius wrote another letter to inform Abby that his grandmother had died, and Abby penned a proper note of condolence.

Toward the end of October a letter came from Rose. Abby eagerly tore open the envelope.

My dear friend, Abby,

As you will see by my return address, I am not married.

I have not been able to write because I have been so full of grief. I must tell you quickly and be done with it. William was thrown by a horse just two days before the wedding was to take place. His neck was broken and he was immediately gone. If it were not for my faith—and his—I could not go on with life.

My one pleasure was to see your Daniel when he and Joshua brought your paintings. When I asked Daniel how you were faring, his color deepened so that I nearly laughed for the first time in months. What have you done to the poor man?

Abby swallowed with difficulty. The proper question was: what had he done to her! She read on. Rose was offering to return the paintings, much as she loved to see them.

They distract me from grief to your great adventure. I have returned all the other wedding gifts as is proper and will try to find a way to ship the paintings so they will not be damaged.

Abby immediately answered Rose's letter.

You must keep my poor pictures if they give you pleasure. What gratification it will give me, dear Rose, to do that much for you now!

After she signed her name, she added a postscript.

As for Daniel, I don't believe that I have had much if any lasting effect upon him. The only help for me is that I try never ever to think of him.

Autumn's fiery colors faded to a stark landscape that was at last transformed to white beauty by December's first snow. Abby's spirits lifted as she sketched the family's snow-covered log house, their first sleigh ride of the year, and the church shining pristinely under its snow-encrusted roof. Even in winter, work in the house kept everyone occupied until bedtime. Aunt Jessica and Rena had been teaching Abby to bake and cook, and in the evening by the fire she helped with the sewing; they were now making durable clothing that would last on the trip, much of it of homespun and even of buckskin for the men. Abby completed the small oil paintings she was copying from the portrait of Grandmother Talbot for Christmas presents.

Two weeks before Christmas, Abby received an odd, rambling letter from Cornelius. Deciding that he must be lonely, she responded with a note about winter life on the frontier. She tried to strike a cheerful tone, telling him how different life was here; he would be amused that the New Year's Ball would take place at the Independence Courthouse, the most elegant building in town. She thought that Horace Litmer might have invited her to the ball if she were not in mourning.

Two days before Christmas, Uncle Benjamin and Jeremy cut a tree in the snowy woods and carried it home by sleigh. Homemade gifts were being readied, and most of the festivities centered around the church. The candlelight Christmas Eve service in the church was so lovely that Abby held the scene in her memory until she could capture it with her watercolors. And Christmas Day was so heartwarming that she thought if she could only erase all thoughts of Daniel and the trip West, she would be content.

On New Year's Day Uncle Benjamin said at the supper table, "I have the great honor of announcing a betrothal."

Abby's heart plummeted. *Rena and Daniel!* Yet Rena asked, "Who is it, Father?"

Uncle Benjamin said to the hired girl, "Now, Sarah, don't run off to the kitchen!"

Sarah blushed. She was a plump, red-cheeked farm girl whose parents and younger brother had died of cholera the year before, after which the Talbots had hired her, though they treated her as family.

Uncle Benjamin stood and took Sarah's hand happily in his. "It is my pleasure to announce that Samuel Schlatter has asked Sarah to be his bride."

Applause and best wishes followed, as the family tried to hide their astonishment.

"Moreover," Uncle Benjamin continued, "they want to accompany us to California. They would like to have their own land to farm. Reverend Thompson will marry them next month."

During the next few weeks Aunt Jessica helped Sarah make a wedding dress and arranged for a small reception in the house after the wedding. Sarah was overwhelmed and confessed in tears, "Never thought a man'd want one so fat like me ... 'n then yer better'n my own to me!"

Samuel was dark and raw-boned, as thin as Sarah was plump. Despite his taciturnity, he was apparently as in love with her as a man could be. Their wedding was small, but Sarah's gratitude at being loved made the ceremony especially touching.

In February, the meetings of those traveling to California and Oregon by covered wagon became more frequent, and trip preparations began in earnest. Uncle Benjamin was having six covered wagons built in town: one for him and Daniel; another for Martha, Luke, and the twins; another for Aunt Jessica and Betsy; another for Rena and Abby; another for Jeremy and Jenny; and last, one for Sarah and Samuel, who would cook and drive their wagon.

At the meetings they often read from guidebooks. *The Hastings Guide* promised, "In California, perpetual summer is in the midst of unceasing winter; perennial spring and never failing autumn stand side by side, and towering snow-clad mountains forever look down upon eternal verdure." One could harvest sixty bushels of corn per acre, it said, and the soil "grows everything—tobacco, rice, cotton, crab-apples, plums, strawberries ... peaches blossoming in January, such grapes as you cannot believe in."

In March, Horace Litmer gave notice to the school board; he too was joining the Talbot wagon train to California. He explained to Abby, "I want to be a real part of history instead of merely teaching it. With Polk as president, 1846 will be a great year of decision. We'll take the Mexico Territories in Texas and the Southwest."

"But what will you do there?"

"Teach if I must." He grinned. "But my great ambition is to print a newspaper. How does *The San Francisco Bay News* sound to you?"

"Wonderful. I had no idea—"

He nodded. "We all have our secret ambitions."

At least he was not emigrating because of her, she thought with relief. He had not even asked whether she was going. Apparently he assumed that she would, and she had never refuted the assumption. Possibly she could remain in the house when Inga, Adam, and their five children moved in, but that would be an imposition upon them. It was one thing to live in the household of an elderly aunt and uncle, who were both widowed, and quite another to live with a young family.

In early April, spring sprouted across the countryside. One Saturday as Abby reveled in the warmth of the sunshine as she swept the front steps, she became aware of someone's presence, and looked up to find Daniel's blue eyes gazing at her. The broom fell from her hands, clattering against the wooden steps.

Daniel returned the broom to her with a broad smile. "Happy springtime, Abby!"

When she did not answer, he added, "Have I been away so long that you don't remember me?"

"I remember," she replied, bittersweet joy returning like the cloudburst on that fatal day in the barn. "It's just that . . . we weren't expecting you so soon."

"I hope that I'm welcome."

She stared at him, torn between succumbing to the warmth of his smile or retreating before she could be hurt again. "I'm sure that you're always welcome."

"Are you still angry with me, Abby? You have no idea how much I regret—"

To her amazement, she blurted, "The oak tree is still charred!"

"I saw it," he responded, backing away, "but it *is* alive."

What is that supposed to mean? she wondered while blood surged to her cheeks. "Everyone will want to see you." She hurried up the steps and quickly opened the door. Her voice sounded hollow as she called out, "Daniel's here, everyone!"

"I'm very sorry about what happened, Abby," he said before the others came running. "You can't imagine how often I've—regretted it."

And you can't imagine how often I've tried to forget! she thought before saying, "I have regretted it myself."

Rena rushed toward them, beaming with pleasure, and threw herself into his arms. "Oh, Daniel, what a wonderful surprise to have you here early! We've all missed you so much."

Abby turned away in anguish.

The emigrants elected Benjamin Talbot captain of the wagon train and began meeting weekly. Abby took more notice since her interests were now clearly at stake. One evening the topic turned to the question of hiring an experienced guide. Someone asked, "Do we need one? So many wagons are settin' out this spring that we could follow their trail."

"It'd be a savin'," another man added.

Uncle Benjamin cleared his throat. "It wouldn't be much saving if we followed the wrong trail. Frugality has its place, but not in this undertaking. I've been as far as Fort Laramie myself, and I kept a sharp eye

out, but nowise would I go without a qualified guide.''
He turned to Daniel, who had been sitting back on the
sofa, quietly taking it all in. "Daniel here has been all
over the world. What's your opinion on this?''

"We need a qualified guide," he replied, "and I
think we should discuss the suggested contracts in the
guidebooks.''

Joel Graham asked, "But isn't signing a contract
about rules taking matters too far? We've chosen our
fellow passengers to avoid the riffraff and despera-
does.''

Daniel said, "A community needs rules to live
by—"

"But we'll be away from civilization!"

."All the more reason for regulations," Daniel
replied. "We will be far more dependent upon each
other than people usually are. We'll be a community
on wheels. Even the guidebooks suggest contracts.''

At breakfast Abby heard that they had voted to
have a guide and signed a contract, which included no
gambling, no drinking of alcohol, and no traveling on
the Sabbath. And they had adopted suggestions from
the guidebooks to promote fairness, such as rotating
wagons. Every day the lead wagon would move back
to the rear of the line so the front oxen would not bear
the brunt of breaking trail through brambly country,
nor would the same rear wagons forever eat dust.

On Sunday morning, Abby did not attend church.
Her heart ached over Rena and Daniel—not that they
acted differently, but that they were always together.
She had just sat down in the kitchen to butter a slice
of bread when a knock sounded at the door. Sunday
morning visitors?

Opening the door, she was astounded. "Cornelius!"

He doffed his hat and stood smiling at her, his
flaxen hair and mustache gleaming in the midmorning
sunshine, his gray suit reflecting the latest in Eastern

styles. "I know it's too early to be calling, but I hoped you would be home. I–I trust you received my letter."

"Your letter?" Abby asked, trying to collect her wits. "No, I have not received one recently."

His smile faded. "It should have arrived last week."

"No. The mail is terribly slow. And one never knows if a letter has disappeared in a steamboat explosion enroute."

His gray eyes held hers. "Won't you invite me in?"

"Of course, Cornelius." She opened the door wide. "It's only that I'm so dumbfounded to see you here."

"I thought you might be afraid of me . . . because of that time in your parents' garden. I assure you that I have very thoroughly repented of that evening. I hope you've forgiven me."

"Yes. And I am sorry too. I shouldn't have led you on like that. It was an intolerable thing to do."

He smiled dolefully. "I didn't require much leading on. However, I've learned that being a roué is not for me."

"I see." She was so unnerved by the direction of their conversation that she scarcely remembered her manners. "Let me take your hat," she finally said. She set it on the entry shelf. "Would you like to sit in the parlor?"

"Yes, if we may." He appraised their surroundings. "It is rather rustic with log walls inside, isn't it?"

"Yes, rather rustic." She marveled at such an understatement from him. "But I've become accustomed to it."

"After your elegant life in New York, I thought you might be suffering cultural deprivation."

A laugh escaped her. "Everything seemed picturesque at first, but the family has been very kind to me, accepting me as if I belong. I've come to feel at home here."

121

Arriving at the parlor he asked, "Is no one else at home now? Do they leave you alone?"

"I—I begged off church this morning since I've been a bit unwell. Here, won't you sit on the sofa?" She settled at the far end and folded her hands on her black cotton dress with forced calm.

He sat nearer to her than she had anticipated, his gray eyes shining with admiration. "You grow increasingly lovely, Abby. I often recalled how beautiful you were last spring, but either my memory doesn't serve me well or you've become more beautiful still."

"Now, Cornelius!"

He sat back and smiled at her with pleasure, then his long face turned serious. "I do wish that you had received the letter. I had counted upon it t-to break the ice, so to speak."

"I'm afraid that I don't understand."

He rearranged his feet on the rug nervously. "The truth is, Abby, that I am not in Independence simply on bank business. As you know, my grandmother has passed on . . ." His eyes darted to her hands as if he might like to hold one. "The fact is that you and I have known each other for a long time, and I have become accustomed to being your friend . . . not to mention other facets about you that I discovered last spring."

"Cornelius!"

"I know a gentleman should not bring it up, but I will never forget. You are very desirable! Since you left, I've thought of nothing but you day and night. I can hardly get my work done at the bank!" He stopped and swallowed with apparent difficulty, finally continuing in a calmer tone, "I have discussed my feelings for you with my parents, and they are quite in accord with me—"

"Cornelius, I—"

"Abby, dear, I beg you to allow me to finish, though this is not coming out at all as I had planned."

She nodded uncertainly.

"The fact is that I can't bear your emigrating to California . . . and my never seeing you again," he said with renewed ardor. "I can't bear your not being in New York with me, Abby. What I am trying to say is that I devoutly hope you will marry me, that you will be my dear wife."

Abby's lips parted. "Oh, Cornelius—"

"I love you, Abby. I love you very much. I promise that I would be a good husband. We can live with my parents in the house on Union Square. My mother is very fond of you, and they are both very pleased at the idea. We could be married here immediately and have our honeymoon in New Orleans and then take a coastal steamship back to New York, or we could be married in New York. My parents are agreeable to either. If you like, they would give us a big wedding in New York, although I would prefer to marry you as soon as possible. I know that you are in mourning, but I understand that traditions are much more flexible here on the frontier."

She was struck speechless. Cornelius was asking to marry her . . . to take her back with him to New York . . . and she would not have to go on the covered wagon trip to California . . . nor suffer as she watched Rena and Daniel.

"I'm deeply moved, Cornelius," she began, "but it is such a surprise to find you here to begin with. I'm still unable to take it all in."

He caught her hands in his. "I love you, Abby. Even if you don't love me yet, perhaps in time you will. I've thought of so many wonderful things we could do together."

She heard a sound at the front door, but in her confusion it flew out of her mind. Here she was sitting with Cornelius, her hands in his damp, cold grip. "What about the scandal?"

"I care nothing about it, Abby. I only want to love

123

you and hope you'll love me. I have taken a fine room in Smallwood Nolan's hotel here in hopes—"

Someone cleared his voice loudly behind them, and Abby spun around with Cornelius. "Daniel!"

"Yes! And apparently at precisely the right moment!" He glowered at Cornelius. "Either leave this house immediately, Adams, or I shall throw you out!"

"I beg your pardon?" Cornelius replied.

Abby leapt up, wide-eyed with disbelief. "Daniel, what are you saying?"

His color deepened. "I heard quite enough to know what he has in mind. Of course, he doesn't care about creating a scandal! This—this degenerate would leave town in no time!"

"Degenerate!" Cornelius repeated, his eyes wide.

Abby faced Daniel with indignation. "Then you certainly did not hear all of it! Moreover, I can't imagine why you should care!"

The color faded from Daniel's face, but he held firm.

"Come, Cornelius," Abby said, "I think that perhaps we should go for a walk."

The front door opened, and the others returned from church. Uncle Benjamin, appearing as astounded as she had been, remembered Cornelius from New York, and Abby introduced Cornelius to Aunt Jessica, Rena, and Betsy. If they realized that they had arrived at an awkward moment, it was not apparent. Indeed, Betsy asked, "Are you one of Abby's beaus from New York?"

"Betsy, what impertinence!" Aunt Jessica admonished, then said to Cornelius, "I do hope that you'll have dinner with us. Your family was so gracious to Abby during her difficult time in New York."

"Thank you," he replied, casting a questioning glance at Abby, who nodded almost imperceptibly. "I am pleased to accept."

Abby said, "And now, if you will excuse me while I get my cloak, we were about to take a stroll."

When she stepped from her room into the hallway, Daniel awaited her with a stern expression. "I hope that I misheard him, Abby."

"You most certainly did!" she retorted. "You arrived in the midst of a conversation and jumped to a conclusion!"

His countenance softened only slightly. "Then you have my apology."

"Thank you. Please extend your apology to Cornelius as well."

"Yes. Yes, I shall."

She started past Daniel, and he caught her arm. "As for your assumption that I would not care, you are mistaken."

She pulled her arm away. "I see no evidence that you care much about me."

He grabbed her shoulders and exclaimed, "I care far too much!" After a paralyzing moment, he unhanded her as if shocked by his own vehemence.

Abby fled down the hallway, the lingering warmth of his touch burning into her flesh, her thoughts roiling. *And what of you and Rena?* she very nearly flung back at him.

Considering the gravity of the men's misunderstanding, dinner and the remainder of the afternoon passed congenially, and afterward, Rena and Daniel departed for a visit with friends.

Before Cornelius left, he pleaded with her at the doorstep, "I shall only be here this week. Please, dearest Abby, say that you will marry me. I don't even see how I shall manage to do the bank's business here with you constantly on my mind. I must know soon. Otherwise, it is only a matter of weeks before you would leave for California—"

He was so overcome with love and concern that Abby held her hand to his cheek. "My dear friend, Cornelius, I am truly honored. And I will let you know as soon as I can sort out my feelings."

His gray eyes darkened with distress. "Do you love Daniel?"

"Why, what an idea! Everyone has always expected that he and Rena will wed."

"Perhaps," Cornelius replied, "but I can see that he loves you."

"Really, Cornelius!" she objected.

He managed a forlorn smile. "I suppose it's only that I am jealous over any man who looks at you."

When he tried to kiss her, Abby ducked her head and his kiss was planted upon her forehead. "Please," she whispered, "you must not be so—so—"

"Passionate?" he inquired with a wry smile.

She nodded. "Yes."

"I shall try," he said as he backed away, "but with you so near it is almost impossible."

When she returned into the house, she felt Daniel's questioning gaze upon her and she hurried away to her room.

At midweek she had still not given Cornelius his answer, and she knew why. She did not love him.

Finally, she attempted to let Cornelius down as kindly as possible, but he said, "You love Daniel, don't you?"

Contrite, she nodded. "Oh, Cornelius, I wish I loved you instead!"

"How I do too!" At length he asked, "And you will go to California?"

"Yes," she decided. "Yes, I will go." No matter how hopeless her love, no matter how terribly it hurt to see Rena with Daniel, no matter how awful the covered wagon trip might be across prairies, deserts, and mountain ranges, she would at least be near Daniel.

CHAPTER 13

THE BEST WAGONWRIGHT in Independence delivered the Talbots' six covered wagons a week prior to their date of departure, much to everyone's joy and relief. As the family hurried out to inspect them, Benjamin Talbot said with a glow of pride, "They are the finest wagons made for our purposes anywhere in this country."

Each wagon was solidly built of well-seasoned ash with elm wheel hubs, oak spokes, wrought-iron reinforcements around the tongue and hounds, wheel tires of iron, and five hickory bows arching over the wagon-bed to support the canvas cover.

Abby and Rena climbed up into their wagon, Rena exclaiming, "Just the smell of this fresh wood makes it seem exciting! You're going to enjoy the trip, I know!"

"I hope so." Abby ran her fingertips over the gray painted canvas that would be their walls and roof for endless months. Inga and Adam had invited her to stay on in the homeplace with them, but it did not appeal to Abby to remain behind like an old maiden aunt, nor did she relish living near the raucous town of Independence forever. She had insisted upon paying five hundred dollars of her pendant money for provisions; Uncle Benjamin had refused more, saying he would have taken six wagons in any event.

"Why are you so excited about going?" she asked her cousin.

Rena blinked in surprise. "Because I believe it's God's will for me to go, that I am to be part of Manifest Destiny."

And I am simply going to be near Daniel, Abby thought ruefully, wondering whether the others suspected her motive. Ironically, Daniel had been keeping his distance from her.

All week long, the sight of the wagons standing between the house and the barn renewed everyone's vigor in their final preparations. There were barrels, some new from the cooper, to fill with flour, salt, bran, cornmeal, water, and molasses, and a new tar bucket for each wagon to hang on the rear axle to grease the wheels and the kingbolt.

In the kitchen, Aunt Jessica directed the work with a calm that belied the excitement sparkling in her brown eyes. "Store the eggs in the cornmeal barrel against breakage . . . the hams go in the bran where they're safer from the heat." Outside, she wrapped her lilac and rose roots in moist soil and newspapers herself.

The evening before departure they packed the barrels, sacks, and boxes of provisions into the covered wagons: sugar, coffee, tea, lard, baking powder, dried fruit, sides of bacon, sacks of dried peas and beans, smoked beef, and two hundred pounds of flour per person. It seemed that Uncle Benjamin had emptied his trading post of trinkets to trade with Indians enroute: beads, knives, fishhooks, colorful handkerchiefs, and mirrors, one of which Abby hung from a hickory bow in the wagon for her and Rena's use.

In addition, there were boxes of ribbons, bolts of cloth, and other light goods to begin the Talbot trading enterprise in California. The plan was to carry enough to begin trade near the Bay of San Francisco, then a Wainwright ship full of goods would arrive before Christmas to continue the venture.

They also carried gold. Daniel had accompanied Abby to the bank to change her remaining money into gold, their outing rather cool in comparison to the previous trip with its stormy passions. Later, she had sewn the gold pieces into her featherbed mattress. She hazarded a guess that Aunt Jessica and the other women had done the same with at least some of their funds.

They also carried tools and garden implements, lanterns, canvas tents, rifles, shotguns, and furnishings that ranged from the small paintings of Grandmother Talbot that Abby had copied to Aunt Jessica's rocking chair.

The sun set with streaks of orange brilliance as Abby attempted to pack the spinning wheel among the boxes and barrels in the wagon she and Rena would share. She knew she had passed a point of no return.

"May I help you with the spinning wheel?"

Abby whirled toward the front of the wagon at the sound of Daniel's deep voice. He wore trail clothing that emphasized his broad shoulders and narrow waist: a coarse hickory shirt and homespun trousers tucked into buckskin boots. With his beard, he made a handsome frontiersman. "Yes, I can't seem to wedge it in here."

He climbed up into the wagon and pressed carefully past her. Taking hold of the spinning wheel, he tilted it between the barrels and a leather trunk. "Pack extra blankets around so it isn't damaged," he suggested.

She nodded. "Yes, thank you, I will."

He stood gazing at her, and she swallowed at the lump forming in her throat. After a moment she said, "I don't see how everything will fit."

"I'm sure that we will manage. The thing that surprises me most is *your* fitting in on this trip."

"What makes you say that?"

"I thought you'd succumb to the pleasures of living the Union Square life in New York. From the look of Cornelius, it wasn't due to his lack of trying."

You are the one who spoke of love's needing to be like stealing fire from heaven! she very nearly blurted. She had truly tried to love Cornelius, but it had not taken hold. When she saw that Daniel awaited her reply she pointed out rather heatedly, "I don't believe that is any of your affair."

He chuckled. "That must be one of the replies taught at Miss Sheffield's."

She raised her chin. "I'm sure that I did not learn it there. I've probably forgotten half of what I learned at school already."

"Good," Daniel said with continued amusement.

She hurried along with him to the house in the last rays of the sunset, resentful of his amusement, particularly as they passed the charred oak tree. The tree evoked memories better left behind, and, from the somber expression suddenly crossing Daniel's face, she suspected that he shared her still vivid remembrance of those kisses.

In the kitchen, a huge pot of stew simmered, its aroma mingling with that of the apple pies cooling on the table. Aunt Jessica said, "If little old Grandma Graham can be cooking and baking pies to the last minute, so can I!"

Abby smiled at the thought of their energetic but elderly neighbor going to California. "I've always wondered how she gets to church on Sundays!"

"She has great faith," Aunt Jessica replied, "and she believes that the Lord wants her to go on this trip."

Manifest Destiny again, Abby thought, then found Daniel looking at her. As her eyes met his, he smiled and turned away with a trace of embarrassment. What did he think when he gazed at her like that?

Uncle Benjamin joined them in the kitchen. "The oxen and wagons are ready."

Aunt Jessica removed the stew pot from the fire and set it aside to cool for tomorrow's nooning, the name given by guidebooks for the midday meal and rest. "We all had better get some sleep. I've already sent Betsy and Rena off to bed."

They bid each other good night despite the early hour, and, as Abby headed for her room, she was aware of Daniel just behind her on his way to the other guest room.

No . . . she must not begin to hope about him again!

The next morning they rose before dawn to partake of Inga's huge farewell breakfast. Outside the windows, the bullwhackers yoked oxen into teams, hitching three teams to each of the covered wagons.

After breakfast Uncle Benjamin summoned the family into the parlor. "Shall we join hands and pray?" he suggested.

Abby found herself holding hands with Rena and Daniel, though there was no time to consider the irony of her position for Uncle Benjamin immediately began.

"Dear heavenly Father, we come before Thee with praise and thanksgiving . . . praising Thee for Thy love for each of us . . . thanking Thee for the blessing of sending Thy Son, the Lord, Jesus Christ, here to earth to be our Savior and to show us how to live. We ask that Thou wouldst keep Adam and Inga and their children here in this house in good health and safety. And we ask for Thy guidance and protection on this journey to California. We pray that Thou wouldst not only guide our footsteps and those of the oxen, but that Thou wouldst guide us in our thinking and speaking so that we might truly be Thy workers in overspreading the continent with Thy Word and Thy love. We pray in the name of Thy blessed Son, the Lord, Jesus Christ. Amen.''

"Amen," Daniel and Rena echoed fervently.

Outside, heading for the wagons, Betsy said, "Abby, you look so pretty!"

Abby blushed with pleasure, noting that Daniel's eyes also examined her. "You're not wearing black!" he remarked.

"Aunt Jessica thought that I might come out of mourning a few weeks early for the trip." She lifted her blue calico dress slightly to avoid the mud caused by last night's rain. The bright color of the dress and her new dark blue cotton cloak had raised her spirits; moreover, she and her aunt had sewn several other colorful dresses for the journey.

Daniel said, "Your dress is very nearly as blue as your eyes."

Taken aback by his open admiration, Abby could think of no reply. She and Rena climbed up onto their wagon and her cousin dimpled in a smile. "It *is* good to see you out of black at last, and you do look beautiful."

"Thank you," Abby responded, more than a little bewildered by Rena's generous spirit. Wasn't she at all jealous of Daniel's notice of her? Her sweetness seemed unnatural. Abby noted that Rena had placed her Bible near at hand, while her own—the family Bible from New York—was packed in a box.

Out along the roadside a few other wagons with fellow emigrants awaited them. Uncle Benjamin, Aunt Jessica, Daniel, Martha and Luke and their twins, Jeremy and Jenny, Betsy, Rena, Abby—all of the emigrants—bid a final tearful farewell to Inga, Adam, and their five children.

Inga called out, "We see you again!"

"Yes!" Abby replied brightly from the seat of the covered wagon. She felt an even deeper anguish, certain she would never return to the comfortable log house that had become a home for her in the past year.

Benjamin Talbot raised his bullwhip and snaked it out into the air with a resounding crack. "Wagons, ho-o!" he bellowed excitedly as he had heard countless others do in past years' departures from Independence.

The weight of the sturdy Durham oxen's shoulders fell against the yokes, and the wagons creaked, then lurched forward. A cheer rose from all around, but Abby simply waved and tried to smile at Adam's family and the friends and neighbors who had assembled to bid them farewell.

Rena mused, "I wonder whether we shall even see California."

"Rena! What a notion!" Abby exclaimed.

"I'm sorry," Rena apologized with a shake of her head. "I can't imagine why I'd say such a thing."

It *was* odd for Rena to raise such a negative thought, Abby mused. At length she set it aside to fix the scene before them in mind for sketching: Daniel and the Talbot men riding on horseback leading the way . . . homely oxen pulling the rolling covered wagons . . . hired bullwhackers walking beside them, cracking long bull whips just above the beasts' backs . . . the log homeplace disappearing behind them with family and neighbors waving tearfully.

Grieved at leaving and newly reminded of the grave dangers ahead, Abby was certain that her sketch would not be dispassionate. *The Ache of Leaving* seemed an appropriate title.

As the Talbot wagons turned onto the muddy side road and passed other covered wagons, waiting to follow them, women and children waved from their seats with excitement. Dogs barked, oxen lowed, and everyone shouted. Little Grandma Graham called out, "I baked ten pies last night!"

From the wagon in front of them Aunt Jessica

replied over the commotion, "You're putting us all to shame!"

Grandma Graham laughed with delight, as did her family. Her son Joel had been one of the first to sign up to go with the Talbot wagon train. He sat on horseback near his family's two wagons, having brought along his wife, Ina, and their seven children, some nearly grown.

Other friends and neighbors in the wagons called out greetings. There was Horace Litmer driving his own oxen like a common bullwhacker; he was carrying not only trip essentials, but a newspaper printing press and, of course, his books. He gave Abby and Rena a rare smile as they rode by him.

The Talbot wagons rolled slowly. First, Daniel's and Uncle Benjamin's, then Martha's with the twins laughing and waving; then Aunt Jessica's and Betsy's, Abby's and Rena's, Jeremy's and Jenny's, and last, Sarah's and Samuel's, which carried most of the cooking utensils.

Abby and Rena waved at Reverend Thompson, whose proposal of marriage Rena had turned down last fall; he drove the oxen, and his new bride, Angelica, sat on the wagon seat smiling shyly at them. The Dunlaps and the Williamsons, each with one wagon full of children, were farmers from New Madrid, where the great earthquake of 1811 had hit. Behind the wagons, three young men herded the loose cattle, spare oxen, and milk cows.

The jumping-off place, where they would meet the remainder of the wagons for the Talbot party, was only a half-day west of Independence. The first day's travel was considered a breaking-in time for the long journey ahead.

"Let's name our steeds," Rena suggested, and they laughingly bestowed flowery names upon the slow-moving oxen: Daisy, Petunia, Pansy, Tulip, Lily, and Marigold.

134

Their bullwhacker, Thad Zimmer, a young man from a nearby farm, wished to seek his fortune in the far West. He was pleasant, not foulmouthed like most bullwhackers. Because Uncle Benjamin lived in Independence, he had been able to hire better hands than those on wagon trains just passing through; moreover, he knew many of the young men's families and had promised to watch out for their sons.

The morning sun rose higher, its warmth dissipating the early chill. A few of the other families' kin had ridden along to see them off, and they began to turn back home, some vowing, "See ye in California next year!"

As they rolled on, Abby brushed wisps of hair back from her face. All in all, it was a most pleasant morning, even if the seat under her had no springs. After a while she decided to join some of the other women who walked to avoid the wagon's jouncing. The sun shone brightly on the rain-washed countryside as the wagons bumped along past outlying farms where children waved.

The scenery became more beautiful as the wagons rolled through meadows abloom with wildflowers and past wooded groves thick with hickories, oaks, walnuts, and elms in their new spring greenery. Hours later they saw the "jumping-off place" in the distance—a meadow with rock outcroppings—dotted with tents and camps of emigrants waiting for their wagons to be completed and for the saddlers to finish harnesses for their teams. Beyond the meadow, valleys lay serenely between deep blue wooded ridges.

In the afternoon their wagons joined the ten wagons that awaited them. They drove into a half-circle, allowing space for the remainder of the thirty-five wagons that would depart together the next morning. Already minor repairs were required, and several bullwhackers returned to Independence on horseback for forgotten items while the herders turned the livestock out to graze.

Abby, Rena, Betsy, and the twins set out to gather firewood and dry brush and returned with their arms full. Before long Sarah heated up the stew in the cast-iron pot over the campfire, and everyone took up their eating utensils from the grub boxes. It occurred to Abby that she had never before dined upon tin plates. In this setting, however, she did not think she minded.

Uncle Benjamin brought out ingenious folding campstools he had devised for the journey, and they all sat down to eat the hearty beef stew and buttered biscuits, followed by apple pie with thick chunks of cheese.

"Isn't this wonderful!" Betsy exclaimed.

Rena gazed across the meadow. "I feel that I'm already in an earthly paradise!"

By suppertime all thirty-five wagons had rolled in and formed a circle in the meadow, and after supper the newcomers ambled about to meet the others. Abby could not help being curious about her new fellow travelers. In addition to farmers, there were saddlers, coopers, and a gunsmith, and even a few foreigners: a French-Canadian couple, the Jacquemans, who kept to themselves; and the Germans, Hans and Frieda Schmitt, with their three half-grown children.

After supper most of the settlers gathered in the middle of the camp circle. Twenty of the wagons would be heading for Oregon, parting from the California group after crossing the Rockies, and there was much talk about the virtues of each place. "Why it's so wonderful in California," one of the newcomers said, "they say a sick person is a rare sight."

As the sun set, a fiddler and a banjo player struck up a lively tune and soon everyone was singing favorites like "On Top of Old Smokey" and "Old Dan Tucker," ending with hymns "to sleep upon," as Rena put it.

They returned to their wagons and tents by the light of stars and low-burning campfires. As Abby lay down to sleep between her blanket and the featherbed mattress, the words of the second verse of "Fairest Lord Jesus" filled her mind.

Fair are the meadows, Fairer still the woodlands,
Robed in the blooming garb of spring:
Jesus is fairer, Jesus is purer;
Who makes the woeful heart to sing.

After a while she asked Rena, "How would anyone know that Jesus is fairer than meadows . . . fairer than woodlands robed in spring? And how would He make hearts sing?" But Rena had already fallen asleep, and Abby pondered the verse until she drifted off into a sound sleep herself.

CHAPTER 14

"WIFE, WIFE! RISE AND FLUTTER!"

Abby awakened to the words the next morning with a smile. It was Jeremy, calling to Jenny in the wagon in front of them.

Rena laughed from under her covers. "That's how Father used to awaken Mother in fun on those rare occasions when she overslept. It's become a family tradition."

Abby stood up as best she could in the crowded wagon and stretched out her stiffness. How lovely it would be to hear Daniel awakening her with that diverting call!

"What's the weather like?" Rena asked.

Abby peered through the puckering string hole on the back canvas. "It rained in the night, but it's another sunny day."

Soon the entire camp was indeed aflutter for the first full day on the trail, and the smells of campfires filled the cool air, followed by the tantalizing aromas of coffee and frying bacon. Abby stepped out of the wagon into pandemonium: people shouted, cattle bellowed, pots and pans clattered, dogs barked, harnesses jingled. Nearby, Daniel dismounted. "Sleep well?"

"Yes, I did." She had not even dreamed of him for a change. "How was your tent?"

"Handy when it rained. But I prefer to look up at the stars."

"I'd like that too," she said without thinking, then suddenly wondered whether he might misconstrue her meaning. She certainly had not meant to say she would like to have looked up at the stars with him last night . . . though she would have! She noticed that Daniel appeared discomfited too. Was he reading her thoughts? She might have blushed if Sarah hadn't called them for breakfast; instead, Abby rushed on to cover her embarrassment. "What a luxury it is for us to have hired help."

"It appears that we're the only ones who do. We have a great deal for which to give thanks." He noticed Uncle Benjamin getting out the folding camp-stools. "Excuse me. I'll go lend a hand.

Before long, they sat down to a breakfast of eggs, bacon, flapjacks, and buttered cornbread, and Abby enjoyed watching Daniel's pleasure more than she did eating. She was glad too that Rena did not sit by them.

Horace Litmer, who had been invited to take breakfast with them, extended his thanks to Aunt Jessica. Upon leaving, however, he commented wryly to Abby, "I'll warrant that such feasts won't last the entire trip."

"You may be right." She wished he were not so pessimistic, but she was not much of an optimist either.

After draining their tin coffee mugs, the Talbot men mounted their horses, and Benjamin Talbot announced, "It's less than a hundred miles from here to the Kansas River ferry—about a week's travel. After we're underway, Daniel and Luke will do the scouting until we meet our guide at the ferry. I'll be busy keeping the wagons rolling. It will just be the bullwhackers and you women with the wagons.''

Aunt Jessica assured them, ''We'll manage fine.''

Abby added, ''Just keep us away from wild Indians!'' The words had no sooner left her lips than she recalled what had happened to Daniel's parents.

''We plan to,'' Uncle Benjamin replied evenly. ''Most of them won't bother us if we don't provoke them. There's been very little trouble between wagon trains and Indians so far, but I daresay the day will come.''

Daniel's eyes pierced hers as if he could not understand her thoughtless remark. He donned his wide-brimmed hat with a nod and rode off while she gazed after him in remorse. How could she have been so thoughtless?

As the time for departure drew near, eagerness raced through the entire party, and the emigrants called out to each other, giddy with excitement. Finally the snorting oxen were yoked and hitched to the wagons, and everyone awaited Benjamin Talbot's starting shout, for it seemed that now they would be underway in earnest. Daniel, riding by on his mare, called out to Abby and Rena, ''Are you lovely ladies ready to go?''

''Ready!'' they called out. Caught up in the excitement, they began to laugh exuberantly.

At the head of the wagon train, Benjamin Talbot bellowed, ''Wagons, ho-o!'' and cheering burst forth across the meadow.

The lead wagon began to roll, then those behind it, then Thad was shouting at their oxen, ''Git-yup! Git-yup!'' and tugging at the lines. The oxen plodded forward, and their wagon wheels creaked onward.

The sun sent warming shafts of light through the sky, and they rode on across the countryside. All went well during the morning and at their nooning

140

stop, but in the afternoon several oxen still not broken to pull loaded wagons balked and lay down in protest, halting the entire train, while the red-faced bullwhackers struggled to get them underway again. Cattle began to stray and had to be brought back, and the hunting party returned with only a few rabbits.

That evening, after traveling their allotted miles, everyone was bone-tired when it was time to make camp. Even the children in their dirtied linsey-woolsey clothing did not romp about the camp as wildly as yesterday. Still, fiddle and banjo music, and singing of folksongs and hymns rang out before bedtime. Like Daniel, most of the men slept in bedrolls on the ground under the wagons or in canvas tents, allowing the women and children to sleep in the wagons. As they turned in, Abby thought again how she would like to look up at the stars with him.

It was turning into a glorious excursion across the rolling countryside, though wagon train life did take getting used to. At first Abby was stunned that they would not take time to stop to wash clothes, but after several days there was a wagon breakdown and everyone stopped in midafternoon to make repairs. Fortunately a creek was nearby.

Aunt Jessica said, "We can't expect Sarah to cook and do the washing, too." She glanced about to be sure that Betsy was out of hearing range. "Sarah looks too tired, and I'm beginning to wonder if she's not with child."

Martha smiled, "If so, she is not the only one."

Rena exclaimed with delight, "Oh, Martha, how wonderful! What if it's twins again?"

Martha shrugged happily. "I wouldn't mind. Now, don't any of you tell yet."

Jenny smiled oddly.

"You too?" Martha asked, and when Jenny nodded, she added, "I thought maybe so. You looked peaked for a while."

"I was," Jenny admitted, "but I'm fine now. Jeremy and I can't wait to have our own young'un."

It had never occurred to Abby before how lovely it would be to have Daniel's child.

Aunt Jessica questioned the women, and it seemed that Martha's baby was due in September, and Jenny's in August. Both would likely be born on the trail.

Abby, who had never been privy to such talk, was astonished to be asked not to tell. "Oh, no, I wouldn't dream of it!" she replied. She presumed that country women discussed such things more freely; nonetheless, it struck her as peculiar.

They trundled the family's dirty laundry to the creek while Aunt Jessica and Betsy cared for the twins. They scrubbed and rinsed, and, in no time, nearby bushes blossomed with Talbot clothing. Abby felt an odd pleasure in washing Daniel's tan shirt and hoped that the other women hadn't noticed her choosing it.

Martha said, "I think I'll have an entire bath myself!" She stripped down to her chemise and began soaping herself.

The others unashamedly followed suit. After a glance about, Abby pulled down her blue calico dress. Hurriedly soaping herself, she was terrified that the men might arrive. *What if Daniel . . . ? What a thing to think of!* She rinsed off with the icy water and dried herself, though the front of her chemise was quite damp.

When they returned to the wagons, Daniel and Luke were repairing a wagon wheel, and Luke asked raffishly, "Did you ladies wash more than the clothes?"

"Never mind!" Martha retorted with a smile at her husband.

Daniel's blue eyes searched Abby out, then quickly darted back to his work, causing her to glance down at

142

her dress. The dampness of her chemise had seeped through the bosom of her dress. Blushing deeply, she hurried away.

That evening at the campfire gathering, she noted that Daniel stayed at Rena's side, though his eyes often turned to her, making her tremble.

The unusually fine May weather held. Although it often rained at night, the days were as lovely as their musical evenings. Even the most skittish oxen settled to their work, and the men learned to take wagons across stream bottoms. It did seem, however, that the fiddling and singing ended earlier, and the travelers tired sooner.

Late Saturday afternoon they arrived at the Kansas River ferry and Abby shaded her eyes to look far beyond the river at the treeless prairie with its vast expanse of green grass.

Rena said, "It doesn't look so fierce, does it?"

"No. No, it doesn't."

They made camp some distance from the other wagon trains awaiting the river ferry, since tomorrow was the Sabbath and they would stop. The wagons had no more than formed their circle when the sad news was out: "Grandma Graham died during her nap."

Aunt Jessica went to Grandma Graham's wagon to help lay out her old friend, and the men set to work building a coffin. That evening after a solemn supper, they held a service under an oak tree for the old lady. Two other graves with wooden headstones lay under the tree. One read, "Elizabeth Sims, December 3, 1797—May 3, 1845. Dead in Christ on the way to Oregon." The other was marked, "John Burg, June 7, 1820—May 1, 1846. Jesus is the way, the truth, and the life."

At the open grave, Reverend Thompson stood by the simple wooden cross he carted in his wagon. "Let us all say the Twenty-third Psalm."

Abby's voice faltered, and she was certain that she was the only one unsure of the words. *The Lord is my shepherd; I shall not want. He maketh me to lie down in green pastures; he leadeth me beside the still waters.* . . .

God had led Grandma Graham to the edge of the Kansas River to lie in a lonely grave where wolves howled. Abby wondered whether the Graham family was angry at Him. They appeared saddened, yet accepting in their grief as they stood beside the coffin. She was probably the only grown-up who had not visited the Graham wagon to see the little old lady laid out in her coffin, but she could not bear it. As it was, she could imagine her packed in the rough wooden box.

Abby stared at the open grave and the crowd, and suddenly the scene reeled. She could only vaguely hear, *Yea, though I walk through the valley of the shadow of death, I will fear no evil: for thou art with me* . . .

Everything began to whirl. She dug her fingernails into her palms to resist the weakness. . . . *I will dwell in the house of the Lord forever* . . . It brought back the memory of her parents' memorial service.

As her legs gave way, strong arms closed around her. She was lifted, then carried away from the death words and Grandma Graham packed in the coffin and the open grave.

Daniel asked softly after they were some distance away from the others, "Are you all right?"

It seemed a long time before she could open her eyes. "I'm sorry," she said weakly, looking up at him. "I'm so sorry. I couldn't help it. It was the open grave—"

He stood her up on her feet. "I've never seen anyone turn white so fast. You must be terrified of death."

"Why should you say that?"

Daniel held her by the shoulders. "I could see the terror in your eyes. And, then, most people are terrified by what they call the Grim Reaper. What is it that Shakespeare said? 'The weariest and most loathed worldly life that age, ache, penury, and imprisonment can lay on nature is a paradise to what we fear of death.'"

Her arms tightened around his neck.

He patted her back awkwardly. "The apostle Paul spoke of physical death for the believer, the child of God, as being 'absent from the body, and to be present with the Lord.'"

He attempted to step back from her, but she clung to him. "Please, Daniel, I don't want to hear that now!" She held him, no longer simply because she felt frightened, but because she loved him so desperately and yearned to remain in his embrace. "Please hold me," she repeated.

He shook his head. "Abby . . ."

"Oh, Daniel, you must think that I am shameless!"

"No, I don't think you're shameless, only human . . . all too human, and torn by temptations . . . just as I am."

"You . . . torn by temptations?" Her fingers slipped of their own volition under his hair to the soft nape of his neck. "I didn't think so. You always seem in control of yourself."

"Not always," he said huskily, removing her hand from his neck. "I know at this moment how David must have felt in the presence of Bathsheba!"

She did not understand, but in the distance she could hear the others singing a hymn by the gravesite, and then Daniel was firmly extricating himself from her. "Abby," he whispered at length, "you need to know the Lord!"

"How can you say—" Looking at the growing hardness of his expression, it was clear that he did not want her love. She whirled away and ran to her wagon, trembling with the frustration of loving him so . . . only to be scorned again!

Shaken, she remained in the wagon Sunday morning able to hear only the hymns from the outdoor service. In late afternoon, she sat out in the shade of the wagon sketching the rolling hillsides of Missouri with the wagons in the foreground and the Kansas River across the way. She penciled in a small graveyard under an oak tree and entitled the picture, *Grandma Graham's Graveyard*. Was this also the gravesite of her love with Daniel? Was today the end of their love?

Quite suddenly it occurred to her that today. . .today was her eighteenth birthday. Grief caught in her throat. Her eighteenth birthday and life held no more promise than on her birthday last year!

CHAPTER 15

ZEKE WILKES, their mountain-man guide, rode in at dawn, his weathered face wrinkled into a squint, his mangy gray beard and long hair blowing in the morning breeze. "Fergit eatin' 'n le's go . . . ain't no Sunday outin'!" he yelled, his voice as ragged as his soiled buckskin outfit. "I held a place fer yer on the ferry, 'n Injuns don' wait!"

The emigrants rushed from their wagons, tents, and bedrolls into a flurry of activity. Before long the oxen were yoked and hitched to the covered wagons, and Benjamin Talbot bellowed again, "Wagons, ho-o!"

Abby felt like grumbling. Even before breakfast the wagons began to roll down toward the Kansas River ferry crossing. She had to admit that Zeke Wilkes's arrival made everyone bustle. Of course, Uncle Benjamin was still captain of the wagon train, but the bona fide guide commanded a certain tight-lipped respect.

The wagons rolled into a line facing the river, then awaited their turn to cross. Abby did not like the looks of the dilapidated ferry, nor of the disheveled

Shawnee and Delaware Indians who ran it, though in their calico shirts, buckskin trousers, and moccasins they appeared no dirtier or fiercer than those she had seen in Independence. The livestock was already being swum across the rushing river, oxen and cattle bawling, men shouting at them from horseback.

Abby caught her breath as she saw Daniel on horseback leading the livestock. It seemed a precarious undertaking, though no more precarious than the way the dilapidated ferry was carrying the first wagons across. After a while she admitted to Rena, "I don't know how to swim!"

Rena looked up from writing her diary of the journey. "Neither do most of us."

"At Castle Garden in New York City there were two swimming pools, one for gentlemen and one for ladies, but my parents did not approve—" She stopped. "Why am I babbling about New York? You never seem rattled."

"I often am, but I just pray."

"I see." Abby did not care to discuss it. She reached inside the wagon for her sketch pad and settled upon the seat again. After studying the scene, she drew the line of covered wagons waiting to cross the river, capturing her anxiety in the expressions of the emigrants.

Nearby, Hans Schmitt complained, "Ve could have saved money if ve floated ze wagons across behind ze oxen."

Zeke Wilkes returned, "Thet's wut some greenhorns sed last week 'n ever' last one of 'em drowned. Ye wanna see the graves wun we git over?"

When it was their wagon's turn to cross, Abby was glad that Thad, their bullwhacker, was in charge of loading their wagon onto the ferry. Once aboard, she closed her eyes and pretended that she was departing New York with Daniel on the ferryboat crossing the North River. She recalled it vividly—his hand at her elbow . . . his tender smile while he presented her sketching case. Then there had been the train ride to Philadelphia at his side and the blissful night in their suite when he had kissed her good night. Despite all of the commotion around her and the rushing sound of the river, Abby focused her mind on the wonderful memories, not opening her eyes again until their covered wagon arrived on the other side of the river.

Uncle Benjamin and Daniel helped Thad hitch their wet and recalcitrant oxen to the wagon, and Abby and Rena were finally settled with the other covered wagons that had already crossed. The men hurried off to assist the next wagon. It seemed only moments later that Abby heard shouts and a woman's cry from the ferry, "Help him! Help him! He's drowning!"

Rena said, "It sounds like Sarah!"

They craned their heads around the canvas top, but only saw people running chaotically near the ferry. After some time the news came up from wagon to wagon. "It's Sarah's husband . . . it's Samuel Schlatter! He slipped, hit his head on the ferry, and fell off into the river! Luke went in after him, but it was too late—"

Abby shivered and remembered Daniel's words: *You must be terrified of death.* Well, why not! She turned to Rena. "What if this is only the beginning of catastrophes?"

"Oh, Abby, you mustn't think that way," Rena admonished. "It's true we should be careful, but we must do the best we can and then turn the rest over to God."

"And where was God when Samuel drowned?" Abby asked angrily. "I remember Sarah's saying she never thought any man would want to marry her, and how . . . happy she was at her wedding. How could God do this to her?"

Rena replied gently, "We can't say God did this. Besides, I'm sure God sees death very differently than

149

we do. Each of our bodies will someday die. Perhaps in childhood or middle age or when we grow quite old. It seems an ending to us still living on earth, but it is really a glorious beginning with Him.''

"And how do you know?" Abby persevered.

"Because the Lord says so." She reached back into the wagon for her ever-present Bible and, sitting up again, quickly found her place. "John 5:24. The Lord says, 'He that heareth my word, and believeth on him that sent me, hath everlasting life, and shall not come into condemnation; but is passed from death unto life.'"

It did not strike Abby as any kind of proof. Nothing changed the fact that Sarah's husband was dead.

Samuel was buried near a cluster of graves under one of the great oak trees, and Sarah wept brokenly throughout the service. As the men lowered the rough casket into the ground, she cried, "Lem'me die too! I wanna be with Samuel!" She broke away in an attempt to fling herself atop the coffin. The men grabbed her, wresting her from the graveside.

Aunt Jessica reasoned with her, "Samuel would want you to go on, especially now that you're going to have his baby."

Sarah wailed, "I don' care! I want Samuel!"

"I'll ride with you in your wagon, Sarah," Rena offered. "I'll take care of you."

Sarah flung herself tearfully into Rena's arms, and finally Rena led her away from the sad little graveyard and shaken mourners.

Abby watched the two of them depart, stunned that Sarah was going to have a baby in the midst of her sorrow. It was obvious that several other women on their wagon train would also give birth during the journey—just in the Talbot group were Martha and Jenny . . . and now poor Sarah.

The men shoveled dirt into the grave, and Daniel placed a wooden marker at the head, upon which he had carved Samuel's name, birth and death dates, and a simple cross. Watching him, Abby marveled at his fortitude.

"Let's be movin' fast now," Zeke Wilkes shouted, "or we'll niver make the California Mountains afore snowfall."

They had eaten cold breakfasts during the grave-digging, and now they would skip their nooning and drive until dark to avoid losing a day's travel. They went sadly but determinedly to their wagons, and before long were underway. Daniel and the other scouts had already set out into the prairie on horse-back, and now Uncle Benjamin and Zeke Wilkes rode just ahead of the wagons, and a few other men rode beside the wagons as flankers. Despite the usual clamor of departure, Abby heard Sarah's wailing.

The trail through the green prairie shifted from west to northwest, and at last it seemed that everything was proceeding properly. Even the weather cooper-ated, the heavier rains falling at night. It would be 220 miles to the Platte River, about two weeks' travel.

The days began to fall into a pattern. At daybreak the women built cookfires from the wood gathered by the children the preceding evening while the men yoked the oxen and readied the herd for travel. Once they were underway, the mornings were filled with the glorious songs of thousands of birds.

In the evenings, Zeke Wilkes insisted upon tighter night corrals, claiming "Ye cain't be too keerful here." Every wagon tongue overlapped the next wagon, and the rear wheel hub of each wagon was chained to the front wheel hub of the wagon behind it. In the enormous corral, the men picketed horses to prevent stealing; outside it, four guards kept watch over the camp and the other livestock in four-hour shifts.

During the days, Abby and Betsy walked alongside the oxen and wagons, exulting in the beauty of the rolling prairie abloom with wildflowers. In places, scatterings of lupine gave such a blue hue to the prairie's emerald green that it seemed a sea. Among the vast undulations bloomed verbena, indigo, geraniums, wild tulips and larkspur, campanella, sweetbriar, and honeysuckle. At times great fields of clover glimmered with the iridescence of hovering hummingbirds, and occasionally an antelope skimmed over the sea of prairie grasses.

The only Indians they saw came by to trade buffalo skins and moccasins. Abby, too unnerved to approach them, asked Horace Litmer, "Would you help me trade for a pair of moccasins?"

"You want moccasins?" he asked, blinking with disbelief.

"Why not? Some of the other women are buying them, and these leather boots are too hot here."

He raised his brows and drew a deep breath. "I don't think it's seemly for you, Abby—"

One of the Indians sensed a sale and thrust out a pair of moccasins that looked about her size.

Daniel rode past, then wheeled his horse back toward them. "May I help?"

Abby said, "I—I want to trade for a pair of moccasins." She showed him the trinkets she wished to exchange for them.

To her amazement, Daniel spoke in an Indian dialect to the brave and effected the sale. It was obvious that he held no grudge against at least this Indian, despite what had happened to his parents.

"Thank you, Daniel," she said as she took the moccasins.

"My pleasure, Abby." Nodding at her and Horace, he rode on.

Horace began to sit with Abby upon the folding campstools during his spare evenings. "This is indeed a beautiful sight," he said one evening.

"Yes, the prairie is beautiful."

He explained rather diffidently, "I meant the sight of you, here."

"Oh . . . but my skin is so brown and my hair is like straw despite my sunbonnet—" She faltered with consternation. "Worse, I've become ungracious. I do thank you for the compliment, Horace."

He smiled, and she saw his green eyes were engrossed with her hands, clasped in the lap of her rose calico dress. She rose nervously and removed herself from his reach.

Turning at the sound of pounding hoofs, she found Daniel riding in for a late supper. If he had noticed the small drama taking place between her and Horace, he gave no indication. Not that it mattered, she thought as she turned to Horace again. He was a fine man, albeit somewhat humorless and schoolmasterly; moreover, he was within her reach.

Stream and creek crossings, with water high from spring rains, seemed the greatest hazard, though other wagon trains they met mentioned rumors of raiding Pawnees from the north. "Doubt thet," Zeke Wilkes countered, "they ain't got their strength back of the smallpox from ten ye'rs ago, but we'll send more scouts out."

In the late afternoons, they made camp at sites chosen by the scouts for their water and grass. While Abby and the other young women and children gathered brush for the cookfires, the bullwhackers looked to their oxen, often cleaning out their sore hoofs. Men were forever at wagon repairs and unhooking the tar-buckets from beneath the rear axles to grease the wheel spindles. Hunting parties rode out in search of game, often riding back to camp with carcasses of antelopes tied on their horses' flanks.

"Sarah's having spells," Aunt Jessica said one evening. "We'll have to take over the cooking."

Abby helped the women make savory stews of antelope or wild turkey. For suppers, there were hot biscuits, wild greens, and stewed fruit, followed by songs until darkness fell. The next morning they would again travel through the great green swells of prairie. Overhead, clouds dappled the blue sky, and the sun blazed so brightly it bleached the canvas coverings of the wagons.

One afternoon the sky suddenly darkened, followed by three days of storms, reminding Abby of Daniel's passionate kiss, and of the lightning that had split the oak tree. Strange that whenever they had become close, he had afterward scorned her, she thought bitterly.

At length the wagons reached Platte River country, a vast treeless landscape extending to the horizon; only here and there along the wide river, cottonwoods and an occasional willow arched over the water's edge. The wagon wheels screeched in protest over the more arid stretches of land, sending up dust all along the column.

For ten days they traveled westward along the south fork of the Platte, seldom far from the shallow brown river. Between the river and low hillsides, the wagons moved upon an ample plain. "Yer comin' to the real West," Zeke Wilkes announced. "Afore long ye'll be wishin' fer rain."

Outcroppings of rock rose from the hills and bluffs, and the grasses were no longer a spring green. Here and there, the grass had been grazed by buffalo, leaving poor browsing for their oxen and other livestock. Plenty of buffalo "chips" were available to fuel the cookfires, appalling as the thought was. Still, there was no longer wood or brush for firewood, and Abby joined Betsy and the children in gathering the dry chips in her apron.

Once, when Daniel came riding in from the day's scouting expedition and saw her, he rode over. "I never thought I'd see Miss Abigail Talbot of Miss Sheffield's School collecting buffalo chips," he said with a grin as he reined his horse beside her.

"Nor I," she responded stiffly. She hoped he did not realize how much she still cared for him, and the thought of it piqued perversity in her again. "I find that I'm doing a great deal that would have astounded Miss Sheffield."

"Aunt Jessica said you're even helping with the cooking. I'm grateful, Abby. Aunt Jessica is not looking so well lately. I think she is suffering from exhaustion."

"I–I thought so myself," Abby replied, "but we are all so brown from the sun, it is harder to tell when one is ill." She noted his own brown skin; his dark beard's new reddish-gold glint from the sun; his eyes, bluer than ever. He radiated good health, his body so toughened from constant horseback riding that he seemed solid whipcord muscle.

"Hopefully Sarah will feel well enough to cook soon," he said. After a moment, he dismounted and accompanied her to the wagons, leading his mare, while Abby carried her apronful of buffalo chips.

She found her resistance to him melting. "What a charming picture this would make."

He chuckled. "I hope you are sketching all along the way."

"As much as possible."

"May I see the sketches after dinner?"

She turned away, her sunbonnet shielding her face. "If you like." Certainly he would only scorn her again. Still, after dinner, she daubed a drop of *Fleur-de-lis* behind each ear.

At length he appeared at her wagon with Rena and Sarah. "I thought we'd all enjoy seeing your pictures," he said. "I hope you don't mind."

"Of course not." Abby's heart had already sunk at the sight of him with Rena. They were such a striking couple: he, tall and dark, and Rena, small, silvery-blonde, and beautiful. Next to them with their bright smiles, Sarah looked desolate, though thinner since she refused to eat.

Abby brought her sketchbook out of the wagon and handed it to Daniel. "Here they are."

They glanced at the recent pictures along the Platte and of the prairies, most of which she had already colored in during noonings and wagon repair stops. At Daniel's nearness and enjoyment of the pictures, all other thoughts fled. Rena admired the sketches with him, but Sarah peered at them vacantly.

He turned the page to *Samuel's Funeral,* and before Abby could think what to say, Sarah rose up in grief. "Samuel! Samuel!" she cried out as if he might hear her from the heavens, then sobbed wildly.

"I'm so sorry! I should have thought!" Abby apologized as Daniel and Rena led the hysterical girl away.

The next morning Aunt Jessica said solemnly as they cooked breakfast, "Sarah miscarried last night."

Abby felt as if she had been struck. "It's my fault! The picture brought back her grief! Oh, why didn't I think?"

Aunt Jessica shook her head. "You can't take all the blame, Abby. Sarah must *choose* to become well; that's part of the healing in grief. Some widows are inconsolable forever; others realize that they must eventually give it up. Sarah used to be sound and stable; it's surprising that she would be so hard hit."

"She thought no man would ever love her!"

"Yes," Aunt Jessica agreed, her eyes turning to Abby with a curious glint. "Yes, she did."

Abby looked away. "I can understand her heartache." It must be even worse than the anguish she felt at losing Daniel, if that were possible.

"We must pray for her recovery," her aunt said, "and we must continue to pray for Sarah's soul too."

It struck Abby that perhaps they prayed for *her* soul! In any case, she became more aware of the graves they saw along the trail nearly every day . . . and increasingly aware that Daniel seemed to avoid her now, doubtless because she had caused Sarah's miscarriage. Well, she would avoid *him!*

Just before their wagon train halted late one afternoon someone shouted, "Buffalo!"

"Buffalo!" the camp echoed excitedly. There they were! Two great old shaggy beasts grazing on brown grass in the distance!

Zeke Wilkes said, "Old bulls. Let 'em be, the meat's awful. Wait fer fat cows."

The next evening, the hunting party did indeed shoot two fat buffalo cows. The entire camp ate steak, congratulating themselves at having journeyed as far as the land of the buffalo. After dinner, Zeke showed them how to make scaffoldings over the cookfires, and they smoked the leftover meat in long thin strips.

The ford of the South Fork of the Platte was a fierce sight, the river being over a mile wide. There was no ferry, and rumor had it that any wagon stalled in shallow crossing would be quickly swallowed up in quicksand. Unfortunately in the rotation of wagons, Abby's wagon was now in the lead, and Thad would have to take it across. Daniel and Zeke Wilkes were already in the river on their horses, trying to reassure everyone with the old saw about the Platte, "It's too thick to drink and too thin to plow!"

Zeke shouted at her, "W'ere's yer bullwhacker?"

Abby looked frantically about for Thad. "I don't know!" She recalled Thad's confession that he could not swim either.

Zeke yelled, "No time fer waitin'! Take 'er across!"

"Me?" Abby cried out fearfully, eyeing the surprisingly strong current.

"I'll guide the oxen," Daniel shouted from his horse. "You just sit tight! It's not deep!"

"Oh, Daniel, I don't know—" She clutched the seat as he led the oxen slowly into the water. Ripples flowed out from around them as they moved along steadily, the water rising higher and higher until the wagon was well into the river. Abby felt as if she were riding into a shallow sea.

"What if there's quicksand?" she called to him.

He shook his head. "Don't borrow trouble."

The oxen plodded forward in the water until they were a third of the way across, then halfway, then approaching the other shore. Finally the ordeal was over, and Daniel guided her oxen and wagon ashore, out of the way of the long column of wagons crossing behind. She climbed down from the wagon and stood by the dripping oxen. "Thank you," she said.

"You're braver than you think," he replied before riding off to assist the next wagon.

"I'm not brave at all," she replied, but he didn't hear. With her fears she would never be suited to a man with such strength of character, she ruminated, loving him anyhow.

Much later, Thad arrived with another wagon, shamefaced and apologetic. "It's all right, Thad," she said. "You weren't the only one who was scared."

They angled over to the North Fork of the river and followed it. In mid-June, the country was now more brown than green, except in the river's bottomlands; the animals grazed on the dry grass without complaint. "Sioux country," Zeke told them. "Make yer night corrals tight 'n double guards."

A knot of fear constricted in Abby, and she watched for Indians from daybreak until dusk. The Sioux were known as great warriors, still proud and strong. Nights she began to dream of Indian raids.

Little by little, the trail began to rise; it became so rough that the wagons bumped and groaned, pounding the wheels mercilessly. Every night wagon wheels had to be mended, and the men hammered in wooden wedges to tighten the iron rims. Two oxen had already died, and their hides were cut into straps to tie up weak wheels.

The days turned blazing hot and the nights cool, and mountains showed against the western horizon. The weather was changeable; one day a sudden storm hit, pelting them with rain that, as the temperature dropped, turned into great hailstones that caused even the oxen to bawl. After it was over, everyone was soaked to the skin and the canvas wagon coverings were torn.

When Daniel rode by to see how they had fared Abby said, "Even the oxen are losing weight. Everyone and everything looks so tired and worn."

"You do too," he responded. "Take care of yourself."

As he rode on, she wondered whether he had noticed that her body had hardened from the constant walking. She certainly no longer looked like a young lady of New York society. Worse, she always felt bone-tired.

The next afternoon Abby spelled Thad at driving the oxen since he had stood night guard duty. He never complained, but looked exhausted, and since many now had fevers, it was best for him to sleep in the wagon during the hot afternoons. The oxen were accustomed to following the wagons, and it was usually enough to control them with the reins. As she walked alongside the oxen, they grew restless, and the dogs began to bark. Abby looked about uneasily, then felt the earth shaking.

"Indians?" she cried to the flanking rider passing by.

The man stopped, his eyes widening for now it sounded as if the ground itself were thundering. "Too loud."

"Buffalo!" another flanking rider shouted, struggling to control his whinnying horse. He galloped to a low hill and looked out across the land. "They're coming from the south! Halt the wagons or they'll pound us into the ground!"

"Halt the wagons!" sounded up and down the line. "Halt the wagons!"

Abby tugged at the reins of the oxen, and in a moment Thad rushed from the wagon to grab the reins from her.

"I'm going to look!" Abby called out and ran with others for a nearby hill. Upon reaching the top, she stood catching her breath. A faraway cloud of dust moved nearer and nearer; at last she could make out the mass of buffalo, thundering across the land ahead. "What if they veer toward us?" she asked.

"They'll flatten our whole wagon train!" someone replied.

Riders galloped toward the herd, and Abby saw Daniel and the other scouts arrive, trying to turn the immense buffalo herd away from the wagon train.

On and on came the great shaggy beasts, the ground shaking under their hoofs, the sky above them turning a gritty yellow. Daniel rode forward, and suddenly a huge buffalo at the edge of the herd saw him and halted precipitously. Daniel fired his rifle, and the buffalo seemed to roar with outrage before rushing at him.

"Please," Abby suddenly prayed, "don't let Daniel be hurt or killed! If You exist, God, save him and I promise I—"

For an instant, Daniel's horse stood still and the buffalo was almost upon them.

"Daniel!" she screamed.

At the last moment, he whirled his horse aside. The buffalo ran past him, veering into the herd, starting to turn them before dropping to the ground. A second and third buffalo were shot, and the herd finally turned in a northwesterly direction, their cloud of dust obscuring the afternoon sun, the sound of their thundering hoofbeats slowly quieting.

Abby's heart thundered like the buffalo hoofs. She had almost tried to bargain with God. What would she

160

have promised Him for Daniel's life? What would she promise Him for Daniel? She ran down from the hill, belatedly aware that their cattle and oxen had stampeded in terror.

CHAPTER 16

For two days the men rode out in search of the runaway livestock while the women cooked and dried buffalo meat. Finally the cry, "Catch up! Catch up!" came again. They made ready to start, albeit with few spare oxen, fewer cattle in the herd, and no milk cows for the Talbots—meaning no more milk, butter, or cream.

As Benjamin Talbot called out, "Wagons, ho-o!" Daniel rode down the line of covered wagons toward Abby, his eyes meeting hers.

"I'm so glad you weren't hurt!"she found herself saying.

"I am too," he replied with a brilliant smile, then doffed his hat and galloped away to take up his scouting duties.

If the emigrants seemed exhausted after the buffalo scare, by the time they sighted Fort Laramie toward the end of June, they were nearly depleted. They already knew that Fort Laramie was not a military fort, but a fur-traders' post where they might buy needed supplies, but when they came in sight of the fort and saw buffalo-skin teepees all around, they were astonished. Daniel and the other scouts rode back to the wagons to say the Indians were Sioux, their warriors riding ponies and armed with lances and bows and arrows.

Zeke Wilkes advised as the emigrants made camp, "They're tradin', but watch yer belongin's, mos' likely yer firearms." Indeed the Indians had ponies, moccasins, and skins for trade or sale, and they descended upon the camp for that purpose, though some of them begged for handouts. Two half-naked braves cornered Abby by her wagon the first night, one of them grabbing her shoulder.

"What do you want?" she cried at them.

They grunted, their black eyes taking in everything from her golden hair to her yellow calico dress and her moccasins. "Good squaw!"

Abby tried to break free, appalled at their frank stares. "I am *not* a squaw!"

Horace Litmer hurried toward them, his rifle aimed. "My squaw!" he thundered furiously. "My squaw!"

The brave removed his hand from her shoulder, apparently as astonished as Abby. They backed off and nodded reluctantly, bestowing another admiring glance at her, leaving Abby so lightheaded that she thought she would either swoon or laugh hysterically at Horace's words.

"Thank you for coming to my rescue," she finally gasped.

"I probably seemed a trifle heavy-handed," Horace said with a grin around his lantern jaw. "Nothing else came to my mind that they would understand so clearly. One would think that with all my years of schooling, I could have handled it more intelligently."

Abby summoned a wan smile. "The important thing is that it worked."

"Yes," he agreed. "It was better than having to shoot them."

"Would you have shot them over me?"

He nodded. "I would not have liked to, but I would have to save you, Abby."

She noticed that Daniel was nearby, no doubt having taken it all in. Why couldn't he have claimed her as "my squaw"?

In camp near the fort, they made wagon repairs and those who could afford to do so stocked up on overpriced supplies. The talk at Fort Laramie was about Hasting's Cut-off, a hotly debated route around a great salt lake.

"This is no time to suddenly change our route," Benjamin Talbot declared, and their contingent finally agreed. The wagon train moved on, bound for Independence Rock. The guidebooks advised arriving by the fourth of July.

The trail grew rougher, and they could no longer follow the river. Ten exhausting days of working up and down hills passed before they arrived at the river again. The upper crossing of the Platte was too deep for fording, and they improvised their own ferry system. During the ferrying, five-year-old Eli Tuttle drowned. At his funeral, Abby hung back; some of the others did not attend at all, among them Sarah, Rena, and Aunt Jessica, who were all too ill.

They arrived at Independence Rock a day late: July 5. If their spirits had been flagging, they lifted at the sight of the great gray mass of rock rising in the wide valley. The guidebooks claimed that mountain men had made a tradition of signing their name upon the rock, but as the emigrants climbed from their wagons, they appeared more worried about the pools of alkali water, one of which was called "Poison Lake."

"See that the oxen don't drink that water, Thad!" Abby called behind her. "I'm going to climb up Independence Rock." She was tired of rough country, tired of the drenching storms and eating dried buffalo meat. She would escape to the heights of Independence Rock to sketch. What did it matter that the other women were going to wash clothes? Everything would only be covered with dust again tomorrow!

She hurried away toward the rock, sketch book in hand. Several minutes later she reached the rugged base of the famous rock, determined to add her name to the signatures and to capture the scene from above. She glanced up at the names etched in the hard surface, then began to climb up the slippery rock, holding her blue calico dress high enough to avoid stumbling. As her moccasins dug into the cracks and crevices, she glimpsed a white alkali flat in the distance, huge strangely shaped rocks, and a meandering river.

Daniel's low voice said from behind her, "It's the Sweetwater River."

"Oh!" She staggered in surprise, and he grabbed her arm before she could fall. "I thought I was the first one up—"

His blue eyes held hers, the grip on her arm slackening slightly. "Scouts always have a head start."

Her usual delight at seeing him instantly fled. "If you're implying that's why I'm here, you are badly mistaken. I prefer to avoid you as much as you want to avoid me!"

Daniel removed his hand from her arm. "Who gave you that idea?"

"You! Who else?"

Daniel looked as if he'd been slapped and replied, "I thought maybe it was Litmer. I understand that you're his squaw."

"That is detestable, Daniel Wainwright!" she replied, appalled. "I have never heard you say anything so—so ridiculous!"

"I'm sorry. It was a poor jest."

"Never mind! I don't want to hear any more of your apologies!" Turning from him, she climbed on,

165

furious and trembling. Why did he have to affect her so? And why had she vented her frustrations on him?

Trying to ignore his presence, she attempted to sign her name on the rock with her sketching pencil, which proved inadequate for the job.

"Would you like to use my knife?" Daniel offered with a curious glint in his blue eyes.

Her voice quavered. "Yes, thank you." She accepted it, careful not to touch his broad hand. She turned to the rock and carved her initials and the date: AWT, 1846.

"Abigail Windsor Talbot," he said.

"Yes." Tremulous, she returned the knife, their eyes meeting briefly before he began to carve his own initials: DAW.

Calming herself during the time it took him to carve, she inquired, "What is your middle name?"

"Adam," he replied as he carved the date.

"No doubt as in Adam and Eve."

He gazed into her eyes, causing her to lose her breath. "Yes, as in Adam and Eve . . . in the Garden of Eden."

She saw the flush rise from under his beard, and she remembered the leaf-clad figures in one of her father's books. Blood rushed to her own cheeks, and she was suddenly far too aware of his nearness, of the masculinity smoldering in his eyes.

"If you will please excuse me," she suddenly said, "I would like to be alone to draw now."

He nodded, seeming as unnerved as she. "Yes, of course."

Several minutes passed before she regained control of her emotions and was able to draw. At their circle of wagons, smoke rose from cookfires; to the west, the Rocky Mountains were sharp and high; behind them, black mounds appeared to be grazing buffalo; beyond that, another wagon train wound up the trail.

When she finished the sketch, others from her

166

group were signing their names on the famous rock, and, as she fully expected, Daniel Adam Wainwright was gone.

The next day the emigrants moved on to the valley of the Sweetwater River, deeper into the Rockies. High peaks and ridges surrounded them, but they found easy grades, fine water and grass, antelope and buffalo, and interesting formations for sketching.

Abby kept her mind away from Daniel and on her sketching: Devil's Gate, Split Rock, Sweetwater Rocks, Ice Slough. And Daniel seemed to keep his distance from her.

They traveled along the Sweetwater for nine days, resting on the Sabbath. Raiding Crows from the north were now the danger, and Blackfeet and Snake war parties from the west.

"Our prayers keep them away, Abby," Rena said at their campfire. "Everyone says the wagon trains that observe the Sabbaths are the ones that get through most easily." She was peaked despite her browned skin, and Aunt Jessica looked as if she neither rested nor slept.

Abby placed her hand on Rena's forehead. "Why, you're fiery hot! Rena, you must go to bed!"

She settled Rena in Sarah's wagon with fresh water and a cold, wet compress on her forehead, installing Betsy to take care of her. Betsy seemed slightly feverish herself, and Martha and Jenny could scarcely help, their delicate conditions hampering them. It was difficult enough for them to endure each day's travel.

As the days passed, Abby found herself not only gathering buffalo chips for the cookfires, but cooking the meals as well. She no longer felt healthy and strong, her constant exhaustion far exceeding that she had felt in previous weeks.

One late afternoon after they had made camp, she rushed to check on Rena, who still burned with fever. Seeing Sarah sitting there in the wagon vacant-eyed,

Abby grabbed the woman's hand. "Sarah, we need you to help now. You have to eat and get well. We all need your help!" When Sarah continued to stare into the distance, Abby suddenly lost all control and wailed, "Don't you see, I can't do everything while you sit here in the wagon! I need help!"

Sarah responded by making her way out to the campfire and resuming her old job. "She's mad," Horace Litmer commented. "She might be cooking again, but she's gone mad."

"She's getting well," Abby said. "She has to feel needed, that's all."

Horace said with an undertone of anger, "In the event you have not noticed, others would like to feel needed too!" He turned and headed toward his wagon.

Abby stared after him, stunned. Her treatment of Horace paralleled Daniel's of her, and she hadn't even realized it! She hadn't intended to hurt him. No doubt, Daniel's intentions were the same.

The emigrants trudged on to South Pass, relieved that in the very backbone of the country, the pass was surprisingly like a broad plain. They could not even be certain where they crossed the point where water flowed toward the Pacific Ocean instead of the Atlantic. At eight thousand feet, they found a skim of ice in the waterbucket at daybreak. Distances appearing a mile or two away took a day to reach.

Daniel stopped by every morning and night to see Rena as they started their descent from the pass. Occasionally Abby came upon him holding Rena's hot hand, the two of them looking happily at each other. The sight of it tore at her heart.

One night she heard Rena say, "I love you so, Daniel."

Daniel replied, "I love you too."

Abby hurried away in agony, her suspicions confirmed. There was no hope now!

Several evenings later he caught up with Abby heading for her wagon. "Abby, you can't do everything," he admonished. "You have been driving yourself more than ever. You're going to exhaust yourself!"

"I don't care!" she flared. "All I want to do is get wherever we're going and be done with it! Three people have died of fever in the past week, and half the others are sick! If I'd had any sense at all, I would have married Cornelius and gone back to New York with him, but, no, I listened to your nonsense about love having to be like stealing fire from heaven—"

"Abby, everyone—"

"I don't care!" she cried on the verge of collapse. "I don't care!"

He caught her in his arms and soothed her. "You do care, Abby. You do care, and that's what makes the hurting worse."

"I know it!" she sobbed against his shoulder. "If only I could be tough and hard and *not* care about anything or anyone—" She thrust herself away from him. What was she saying? Aghast, she turned and ran to her wagon. It was her love for him that was destroying her, she thought. *He* was destroying her!

CHAPTER 17

"IF YE THINK SOUTH PASS was easy, ye got another good surprise waitin' terday," Zeke Wilkes informed them at breakfast before they began their descent down the Rocky Mountains. He had begun moseying about the Talbot cookfire now that Sarah was again cooking, albeit in a vacant-eyed daze. Zeke added, "Ternight we make Li'l Sandy Crick . . . nigh on twenty mile."

Abby headed for her wagon. She had decided it best if she tended to Rena now that Sarah was cooking and Betsy was taking care of Aunt Jessica. Last night Daniel had carried Rena to the wagon and helped settle her there.

In the wagon, Abby leaned over Rena who drowsed in her makeshift bed, her face pale. "We're supposed to make twenty miles today, Rena. Isn't that wonderful? You know we've only been averaging fourteen miles a day."

Rena opened her glazed eyes for an instant and smiled, her dimples no longer deep in her gaunt face. "Yes, only a few more miles."

Abby placed a hand upon her cousin's brow. It was already hot! She dampened a cloth and laid it upon Rena's forehead. Her cousin often made peculiar comments now. In the middle of the night, she had laughed happily in her sleep, then uttered, "Oh, yes, Lord! Oh, yes!" It had given Abby such a fright that she had listened to Rena's breathing, unable to fall asleep again for a long time.

Outside, Benjamin Talbot was already calling "Catch up! Catch up!" and Abby asked Rena, "Is there anything you need before we leave?"

Rena's brown eyes appeared less glazed as she opened them now. "Only for you to love the Lord."

Abby stiffened. If her cousin were not so sweet, she would be furious. After all, she had gone to church with them in Independence and to most of the Sunday meetings on the trail, and she was even learning the words to hymns. No matter what she did, it still didn't seem enough to please Rena. "Yes. Well, you concentrate on resting. I'll look in on you often." Trying to soften the harshness in her voice she added, "Daniel stopped to see you before you awakened."

"I thought so," Rena murmured with a blissful smile, and Abby's spirits wavered.

Betsy popped her head in. "Time to leave!"

"I'll be right there," Abby replied.

The girl's green eyes turned with concern to her older sister. "I hope that you'll sleep today, Reenie."

"I'll be fine," Rena assured her. "I'm improving all the time."

Abby did not think so. Outside, she was glad to hear Benjamin Talbot's call of "Wagons, ho-o!" and to start their descent from the heights of South Pass.

The wagon train set out over rough terrain on the downhill trek, reaching the Little Sandy Creek in good time. Abby could not understand how Rena withstood the terrible bouncing in the wagon. Only the sick and injured rode in wagons now, not merely to save the oxen, but because it was infinitely more comfortable to walk. At every stop, Abby changed the wet compresses on Rena's fevered brow.

Fortunately the next day was Sunday, and they made camp near the willows of Little Sandy Creek. Clear water rippled over the fine sand and, though the grass had been trampled by recent wagon trains, sufficient grazing remained for the stock. Abby was pleased to see the oxen rest. "I never thought I'd care about such homely beasts," she admitted to Betsy, "but I hold each of them in great affection now!"

Rena and the other invalids were brought out of the wagons for the creekside Sunday services. Abby watched Daniel carry Rena out tenderly and seat her upon a blanket, then settle at her side. Jenny and Martha, who were now great with child, sat on blankets with their husbands in the shade of the willows, trying to quiet the energetic twins. Aunt Jessica sat with Abby, insisting that she was nearly well again, and Betsy joined them.

Together, in front of the cross Seth Thompson had set up for the service, they sang:

This is the day the Lord hath made;
He calls the hours his own:
Let heav'n rejoice, let earth be glad,
And praise surround the throne.

Abby glanced sidelong at Rena as they started the second verse, marveling again at how her cousin seemed to gather strength as she sang. Last night she had washed Rena's hair and now in the sun-dappled shade of the willows, it shone like silvery silk; her brown eyes brimmed with faith.

Seth Thompson, his sandy hair sun-bleached, spoke of the wilderness through which Moses and the children of Israel had wandered, then referred to the wilderness ahead for each of them during this westward trek and the rest of their lives. "Through all of these wildernesses we must honor God first and

172

foremost," he preached. "We must stand aside, keeping our own sinful natures in abeyance and become holy vessels for God."

Abby did not think herself such a great sinner.

Toward the end of the service Seth requested Daniel to read a passage from the Book of Deuteronomy.

Daniel might have been Moses giving the commandments as his deep voice proclaimed: "Hear, O Israel: The Lord our God is one Lord: And thou shalt love the Lord thy God with all thine heart, and with all thy soul, and with all thy might."

Seth Thompson requested, "And now, please, from the New Testament, the Book of Matthew," and he added the chapter and verses.

Daniel turned the pages of his Bible, the soft breeze tousling the curls of his dark hair and beard. Finding his place with assurance he read, "Master, which is the great commandment in the law?" He paused, and Abby could not remove her eyes from the aura of faith emanating from him. "Jesus said unto him, Thou shalt love the Lord thy God with all thy heart, and with all thy soul, and with all thy mind. This is the first and great commandment . . . And the second is like unto it, Thou shalt love thy neighbor as thyself."

Rena's beatific smile wrenched Abby's heart. How well suited her cousin and Daniel were for each other.

The company sang "Amazing Grace," quieting toward the end of the third verse to allow Rena's melodious contralto to rise:

'Tis grace hath bro't me safe thus far,
And grace will lead me home.

Abby wiped a tear away with her fingertips; the others' fading voices told her they too were touched as Rena sang the fourth verse:

When we've been there ten thousand years,
Bright shining as the sun,

173

We've no less days to sing God's praise
Than when we first begun.

In unison they fervently sang out across the creek banks, filling the camp and the sky: "Praise God, praise God, praise God, praise God . . ." The joyous sound of their praise lingered with Abby long after the service.

In midafternoon Jeremy came running for Aunt Jessica—sick as she still was—to hurry to Jenny's wagon. Before long, the word went from wagon to wagon: "The baby's turned wrong." By sunset, the word went around again, "The baby's lost."

At first Abby's heart constricted, then she was furious. She did not care for this God of theirs! Jenny had wanted this baby! If God existed, He was entirely cruel and unfair!

The next morning, they stopped at the Big Sandy River, where the men cut grass to take along in the wagons, and women and children filled every possible jug, pan, and keg with water. As Abby carried the last of the water jugs to their wagons, she looked to the landscape they would have to cross—a flat, barren tableland, relieved only by occasional clumps of dried sagebrush and rocks. "Never saw anything like it," and "It's sure nothing like at home," she heard again and again.

Zeke Wilkes warned, "There be no water, no grazin' . . . nothin' 'til Green River, 'n thet's nigh on forty-five miles."

The wagon train traveled in a straggly column across the desert, through rocky ravines, and past alkali ponds that glistened in the sunshine with a deathly whiteness. The wagon wheels and oxen's hoofs sent up fine white dust to fill Abby's eyes, mouth, and nostrils. Sagebrush tore the oxen's undersides and stopped the wagons, and the men hacked at it with axes, gasping in the blazing sun.

Zeke called for two watering stops in addition to the nooning, though there were only a few swallows of water for each of the oxen.

The lead oxen, Lily and Tulip, looked weakest, yet they plodded on. *There's no turning back now*, Abby reflected, *only going forward*. Surely California would not be a disappointment after enduring this.

In the afternoon the exhausted oxen pulled the wagons toward the relentless sun. Abby was blinded so that the desert seemed a bright blur. Beside the trail were moldering ox carcasses from recent trains and bones of others long picked clean. Here and there they passed furniture and other goods that earlier wagon trains had thrown out to lighten their loads— heavy blacksmith tools, an old bureau, trunks, and even a rocking chair.

The first day in the desert they made eighteen miles. That night there was no firewood for the cookfires, not even buffalo chips. Coughing, Abby helped them build fires with the greasy sagebrush. All around them the men worked on the unending wagon repairs; the desert's fierce heat had shrunk wheels, tongues and hounds, and even the hickory bows holding up the canvas.

The next morning they found three oxen dead and two others so weakened that they had to be left behind. "Have to shoot 'em," Zeke Wilkes said and did the job himself.

Abby jerked as each shot filled the air. With her throat parched before they even set out, how could their oxen not be suffering? Even the dogs seldom barked here.

At their first water stop, Horace Litmer presented her with a smooth gray pebble.

"What's that for?" she inquired.

"Keep it in your mouth. It helps to make saliva."

She nodded. "Thank you, Horace. What a sorry pass things have come to. I can't imagine what Miss

Sheffield's reaction to this would be." She immediately regretted her words. "I'm sorry . . . I seem to think about New York now to avoid dwelling upon the dryness and dust."

"I didn't think it would be this bad myself," he said, "and I made a study of it. If only there were shade somewhere. Some of our fellow travelers are slaking their thirst by sucking on rags soaked in vinegar."

At midafternoon they passed another wagon train that had stopped to bury a woman—sixty years old like Aunt Jessica—who had died from exhaustion. Despair rushed through Abby to see that the body was only wrapped in a sheet and being buried in a shallow grave.

Wolves tracked them now. At night the guards set sagebrush fires around the perimeter of the camp to keep them at bay. Abby lay wide awake, listening to Rena's shallow breathing and to the wolves' howls.

On the third morning Tulip was dead, and Uncle Benjamin put Lily out of her agony.

"Oh, Abby!" Betsy cried, burying her face on Abby's shoulder and shaking with sobs.

"It's all right, Betsy," she replied. "It's going to be all right." She felt like crying herself.

Rena's fever burned constantly despite the vinegar-dampened cloths on her forehead; she lay frighteningly still and uncomplaining in the heat, resembling a porcelain doll with a waxen face and bright red cheeks.

Just after high noon Daniel and the other scouts rode back, covered with dust and grit. "The Green River!" they shouted. "Just below those bluffs. There's a ferry and pine forests and good streams and springs!"

No one had the strength to even raise a cheer.

When they had finally descended to the swiftly running stream, Abby kicked off her moccasins and waded into the water in her dusty dress. "It's cool!" she called out to Betsy, who joined her.

After the awful trek through the desert, the rugged mountainous trail was what Aunt Jessica called "a blessed relief." A week's travel through high ridges and pine forests brought them to the Bear River, from which they swung northward. The great attractions on this dull stretch were soda springs, whose water tasted like sulphur. When they stopped, Abby and Betsy sketched the springs. Surprisingly, Rena felt well enough to sit outside one evening to write in her diary. When Daniel rode in from scouting he ambled over to join them, carrying his tin plate full of antelope stew.

"Look at Steamboat Spring!" Rena called to him over the chugging sounds of the water. "Doesn't the Lord create wonders?"

Daniel beamed. "Yes, He does." The way he looked at Rena left no question in Abby's mind that he thought Rena one of those wonders. They made a charming picture sitting by the covered wagon and looking out at the spring. Abby did not sketch them into her scene, though she noticed that Betsy did.

It was a dull ten-day pull to Fort Hall, a fur-trading post of the Hudson's Bay Company. They arrived on a Saturday afternoon and settled down to rest, repair wagons, and buy a few supplies while the stock grazed on the green grass.

Benjamin Talbot exulted, "Over halfway to California! We've traveled nearly twelve hundred miles!"

Halfway? It seemed impossible. How could they manage that distance again with the California Mountains more rugged than the Rockies?

CHAPTER 18

On SATURDAY NIGHT THERE WAS MUSIC and, around a blazing campfire, they all sang "Sweet Betsy from Pike" and the other favorites. The evening had a special poignancy since next week over half of the company would split away toward Oregon. Even Aunt Jessica summoned up the energy to join in, a sad-faced Jenny at her side.

Together the group reminisced about their trip—about their first days out, fording the rivers, the Indians at Fort Laramie, the buffalo stampede. Zeke Wilkes, sitting near Sarah, was urged to share something from his years of travel and finally gave in.

"Wun I was a boy, we was south o' the Platte wun we had t' corral our wagins t'keep the stock from bein' stampeded by buffalo," he began. "Six days n' nights forty men kep' killin' buff'lo to keep 'em off the wagons. Nex' day the buff'lo herd spread, givin' us a chance to yoke up 'n cross the Platte, 'n it's a good thing thet we did!"

"Why is that?" Benjamin Talbot inquired.

"Well," Zeke replied, straight-faced, "we no more

'n hit the other side o' the Platte, 'n here comes the main herd!''

Everyone laughed at his tall tale, even Sarah and Horace.

Abby edged away from the campfire circle, taking a good look around for Indians beyond their wagon circle in the moonlit night. Stars blanketed the sky all around. Cattle lowed as they settled for the night, guards called to each other around the corral circle, and coyotes howled eerily in the distance. She returned to her wagon while the others sang their "hymns to sleep by."

She still lay awake on her featherbed mattress when Daniel returned Rena to their wagon, trying not to hear their murmurings. Did he kiss Rena as passionately as he had her? The thought haunted her in and out of sleep all night long.

During Sunday services, special prayers were made by the Oregon contingent for those bound for California, and prayers from the California contingent for those heading toward Oregon. Forty miles later at the Raft River, the groups parted, their members shaking hands solemnly. Gone was the spirit of audacious adventurers setting out on a lark as when they had left Independence in the spring. As the wagons pulled away, the women rallied slightly, calling out to each other. "Now be sure to write so we know how you came out!" and "Maybe we'll see you again!" and "Be sure to come fer a visit!"

Betsy asked, "Do you think we'll ever see them again?"

Abby shook her head sadly. "I don't think it's likely."

"There's only thirteen wagons of us now," Betsy said.

"We'll manage," Abby replied. "We have to."

The California Trail rose southward alongside the Raft River, staying close to a stream, then veered off along another stream. They made camp in the City of Rocks, and, after dinner, Abby and Betsy sketched the twin spires high above their small circle of thirteen wagons, naming their sketches *Cathedral Rocks*.

During the next week, the trail dropped into a wide valley, then climbed another great divide, and dropped again, this time abruptly, to Goose Creek. At night, Indian fires flared on the mountaintops. The Talbot invalids, who now included Rena and Martha, seemed to rally during their next five days' journey toward the southwest. Aunt Jessica said, "It seems to me that the good Lord meant settlers to come this way. Look at how easy South Pass was through the Rockies, and now we have streams all through this dry, rough country. There's water for us and grass for the stock."

Benjamin Talbot agreed. "It does seem providential."

Rena said, "He wants us to tell of His love, to tell everyone on earth of it. I pray that I might be used to help take it to California . . . to take His love westward."

It was now, they said, about four hundred miles to the California Mountains, most of it along the Humboldt River. Abby continued to sketch when she could, although for the most part it was uninteresting country—grass along the streams and desertlike uplands with scatterings of sagebrush and prickly pear cactus. Occasionally the hunting parties brought in an antelope, but more often they shot jackrabbits, which had to be, as Sarah put it, "stewed to death."

"Watch out fer the Diggers," Zeke warned about the next group of Indians as they traveled on. "They're scavengers, 'n they'll steal the shirt off yer back. Ain't got no horses, 'n they live in the dirt. Worse, they'll eat anythin' they lay a hand on, even grasshoppers 'n rats."

Before the day was out, one of the small desert

tribes descended upon them, peering from around rocks and clumps of sagebrush. Occasionally Abby caught glimpses of the squalid creatures and shivered. Dirty as she was herself now, their filth and half-nakedness was appalling. She kept Betsy close to her as they walked alongside Thad and the oxen.

"Pretend they ain't there!" Zeke admonished as he rode his horse along the column of wagons, "but keep yer eyes on 'em too."

When they made their corral that night, it became obvious that they had not watched closely enough. Two cattle were missing. One of the bullwhackers shouted, "We ought to shoot them Diggers . . . teach 'em a good lesson!"

"They have to eat too," Aunt Jessica replied. "They don't know better, and we have to forgive them."

The river and the days seemed endless as they trudged alongside the wagons. As the weeks went on, the emigrants became increasingly disenchanted with the Humboldt, which Horace Litmer renamed the *Humbug River.* "It doesn't even warrant the appellation, *river,*" he said heatedly, "not after one's seen the Ohio or the Mississippi, or even the Missouri. It doesn't run like a river, and no one has seen a single fish in it, nor any other living thing!"

Abby tended to agree. Every day there was less grass for their oxen, and the water turned more sulfurous, a sickly white in color. Along it, they had come into a region of sage, rabbit bush, and scrubby willows near the river bank.

Groups of Diggers continued to dog them. They snatched the emigrants' newly washed clothing from the banks of the Humboldt, and on one dark night, two horses. Several nights later, they stole more cattle. They were difficult to spot, roaming like spectres around the edges of the wagon train.

At dawn one day Rena murmured from her bed in

the wagon, "I would like to tell those Indians about the Lord . . . about how much He loves them."

"Oh, Rena, they wouldn't understand," Abby responded. She felt her cousin's forehead and drew back in shock. It had never before been this hot!

She pulled on her wrapper and rushed outside into the glimmering dawn that was slipping across the horizon. Dipping a compress cloth into the water barrel, she was dismayed to find the water lukewarm. She wrung out the cloth and hurried back into the wagon, folding it for Rena's brow. "Let me wash your arms and legs to cool you off, Rena."

"I don't like to be such a bother," Rena murmured.

Abby peered outside at the emigrants sleeping on their bedrolls near the wagons and was grateful that others were beginning to stir. The cattle guards were riding in, and here came Betsy out of the next wagon to sit on one of the folding stools to braid her hair.

"Betsy!" Abby whispered, "please get us a bucket of cold river water. Rena has a fever again!"

Betsy stopped braiding her hair and jumped to her feet, her eyes widening with worry. "I'll hurry!" She grabbed a bucket and ran out toward the river.

Abby changed into her blue calico dress, keeping an eye on Rena. Now that the sun was rising, she saw that her cousin's lovely face was bright red.

Rena opened her eyes, and they were far too bright, too glazed. "Abby, dear," she began in a faraway voice, "if I go on to be with the Lord . . . promise you'll read the last pages of my diary."

Abby caught her breath in despair. "Oh, Rena! What a thing to say! You're not going to—"

"Promise you'll read them," Rena pleaded weakly. Her pale blonde hair spread across the pillow and a tender smile touched her lips. "I love you so much, Abby."

Abby choked back a sob. "I promise. But you aren't—aren't going to—leave." She fell on her knees and placed her face against Rena's flaming hot cheek. "Oh, Rena, I may not have always shown it, but I do love you! Oh, I do!"

Rena's eyes glowed. "I know you do."

They gazed at each other for a long moment, and Abby's mouth trembled. "Oh, Rena, please get well!"

Her cousin nodded slightly. "Are the lilac and rose roots still moist?"

Abby blinked at the odd question. "Yes, I'm sure they are again now that we're at the river."

After a long silence Rena murmured, "I'd like to talk with Daniel."

Abby rose to her feet in anguish. She peered out the front of the wagon and spotted him. "Daniel!" she called out, waving frantically for him to come, noting the instant apprehension on his face.

As he rode up she could scarcely summon the words, "Rena's asked to see you. She's awfully feverish."

"I see." Dismounting, he quickly tied the horse's reins to the nearby wagon wheel.

Abby clambered down from the wagon. "I sent Betsy for cooler water from the river so I can bathe Rena." It suddenly seemed an indecent thing for her to mention to the man who was going to—marry Rena, and she flushed. "I–I think I'd better get Aunt Jessica to help."

Daniel removed his wide-brimmed hat and climbed up into the wagon. "I'll stay with Rena until you return."

Abby felt uncertain of what people might say of the two of them in the wagon together, but this was no time for niceties. She hurried to the next wagon. "Aunt Jessica?" It was empty. Everyone was beginning to scurry about the camp to get ready for breakfast and the day's trek. She finally spotted her aunt running up from the river bank with Betsy and Sarah.

"Aunt Jessica!" she called out and ran out to meet them.

"Betsy said that Rena's fever is back," her aunt gasped.

"She's terribly hot!" Abby took the water buckets from her aunt. "I'm sure she's never been this bad before."

"I'll help you bathe her," her aunt said. "Betsy, would you please help Sarah prepare breakfast? And ask your father to stop by Rena's wagon."

"Yes," Betsy replied, her green eyes filling with tears. At the wagon she asked, "Can I see Reenie too . . . before—before—"

Aunt Jessica gave her a hug. "Just as soon as we get her temperature down. Now, don't you worry, this fever comes and goes with her."

Betsy appeared no more reassured than Abby felt.

Daniel stepped down from the wagon, looking grim. "I'll ask someone else to scout for me today." He unwound his horse's reins from the wagon wheel and led her away, his other hand on Betsy's small back. "Come on, Betsy," he said to her. "Give me a hand with my horse first."

Betsy managed a tearful smile up at Daniel, and Abby fought back sobs.

Inside the wagon, she and Aunt Jessica constantly changed the wet compresses on Rena's brow and bathed her face, arms, and legs with the cool water while Rena slipped in and out of consciousness.

Before long Jenny arrived with more compresses and to offer her assistance, and then Martha, who could scarcely walk now, let alone climb up into the wagon in her maternal condition. Aunt Jessica opened the back canvas flap of the wagon so they might be near Rena. Martha urged, "You have to get over this fever, Rena. You have to help train my new baby."

And Jenny simply whispered, "Oh, please get well. Please!"

Rena smiled at them with a wondrous love.

After a while Benjamin Talbot came to hold his daughter's hand, his eyes filled with tears. "Now, Rena, you've got to set yourself on getting well."

Her lashes fluttered and she looked up at her father. "You're such a good and loving father," she whispered.

Benjamin Talbot asked, "How could anyone help loving you?"

She closed her eyes in happiness.

He said, "Maybe we shouldn't have come West after all."

She shook her head. "We were to come."

Aunt Jessica said, "Please, no more. Rena must rest."

Benjamin Talbot nodded and led Martha and Jenny away, while hot tears slipped down Abby's cheeks.

At length Reverend Thompson stopped by, Bible in hand. "May I talk to her? Daniel suggested I come."

"Yes, of course, Seth," Aunt Jessica said.

"Rena?" He leaned in from the back of the wagon and took her hot hand in his.

She stirred at his voice, and her eyes fluttered open toward him. "Seth," she whispered, "my dear friend."

He blinked hard and rested his Bible on the wagon gate. "I thought that you might like me to read a bit to you."

She closed her eyes and smiled. "Only after . . . I tell you that I knew . . . I knew . . . Daniel did too."

Knew what? Abby wondered. She quickly looked away from the pastor, who wiped his eyes with his knuckles. It was a while before he could continue. "Would you like to hear something from Psalms?"

"Please . . . John . . . 3."

After a slight hesitation, Seth Thompson found the page, then closed his eyes in prayer before reading. "There was a man of the Pharisees, named

185

Nicodemus, a ruler of the Jews. The same came to Jesus by night, and said unto him, Rabbi, we know that thou art a teacher come from God: for no man can do these miracles that thou doest, except God be with him."

The pastor glanced at Rena thoughtfully, then down at his Bible again. "Jesus answered and said unto him, Verily, verily, I say unto thee, except a man be born again, he cannot see the kingdom of God."

And what does that mean, to be born again? Abby wondered as she continued to bathe Rena's hot arms.

Seth read, "Nicodemus saith unto him, How can a man be born when he is old? can he enter the second time into his mother's womb, and be born?

"Jesus answered, Verily, verily, I say unto thee, except a man be born of water and of the spirit, he cannot enter into the kingdom of God. That which is born of the flesh is flesh; and that which is born of the spirit is spirit. Marvel not that I said unto thee, Ye must be born again."

Rena murmured, "Thank you."

Seth nodded, his voice tremulous. "It is my great, great pleasure, my dear Rena. You—you'd better rest now." He turned quickly, his head bowed as he walked away.

Betsy appeared at the back of the wagon. She whispered with a worried glance at Rena's labored breath, "Papa said that I might come now."

Aunt Jessica nodded.

If anything, Rena was even hotter. Abby thought it impossible for a person's body to become so hot.

Betsy's lips trembled. "Oh, Reenie," she whispered, "I love you so."

Rena's lashes fluttered again, her eyes turning to Betsy. Her voice was soft as the sound of a falling leaf, "I love you, Betsy."

At length Daniel and Jeremy and Luke stopped by, and Rena murmured "I love you" to each of them, to

Abby, to Aunt Jessica. She seemed compelled to give out love, and her words touched them like dewy rose petals, even in the morning heat. Suddenly her body shuddered and was still.

Abby felt her eyes widening. "Is she—?"

Her aunt felt Rena's heart and shook her head.

"Not yet," Daniel said wretchedly and turned away. "Not yet."

As wagon train captain, there was really nothing much for Uncle Benjamin to do but to keep the company moving along at a steady pace, and Zeke Wilkes called them into position for him, then bellowed, "Wagons, ho-o!"

Aunt Jessica insisted upon remaining in the bouncing wagon with Rena, and Abby and Betsy walked disconsolately at its side.

They glanced occasionally toward the Humboldt Mountains, but around them all was desolation— sagebrush and dust.

When they stopped for the nooning, Abby hurried to help Aunt Jessica down from the wagon, for she could not climb down herself. Her wrinkled face was gaunt yet composed, and Abby could not bring herself to inquire.

"How is Reenie?" Betsy asked.

Aunt Jessica's eyes closed. "Rena's soul has been released to be with the Lord."

"No!" Abby cried, throwing herself into her aunt's arms. A sob escaped as if from the depths of her soul, then another and another until it seemed she might never stop weeping.

She had secretly wished for Rena's death! She had secretly wished it even though she had never admitted it! She had wished it so she might have Daniel for herself!

"Abby, you mustn't take this so hard," Aunt Jessica said, patting her shoulder. "Rena is with the Lord."

187

Abby shook her head, feeling as desolate as this hideous wilderness. As much as she loved Rena, something dark and hateful within her had wanted her to be dead! And now because of that terrible terrible wish, she could never in good conscience marry Daniel!

CHAPTER 19

TREMBLING, ABBY STOOD with the Talbots at Rena's desert gravesite. *This cannot be!* she thought, squinting into the blazing sunshine.

The open grave alongside the trail was unreal, a nightmare; indeed, everything in the blinding sunshine appeared surrealistic. She sensed Digger Indians lurking around them, ready to pounce from nearby clumps of sagebrush. *We can't leave Rena here!* her mind screamed at the men as they placed her cousin's blanket-shrouded body in the dusty grave. *We can't leave Rena here!* In the monstrousness of it all, the words refused to travel from her mind to her tongue. Finally she clamped upon Seth Thompson's words: *Ashes to ashes, dust to dust.* That, at least, was fitting for this dismal place.

As the men did their grim duty, throwing shovels of desert sand into the grave, Abby turned away with great gulping sobs. Aunt Jessica tried to soothe her, but to no avail. When Abby at last caught her breath, she saw that she alone was so overcome by grief. The Talbots looked saddened, but not as heartbroken as

189

she. A memory surfaced of Daniel's saying, "You must be terrified of death."

That was not the case here! She was only grieving over Rena. How could the others be so composed? Perhaps they had not loved Rena so deeply.

Betsy turned to Abby. "We can't have a headstone for Reenie."

"And why is that?" Abby asked so sharply that her small cousin drew back.

"It's the Diggers . . . they dig up bodies for clothes."

Abby shuddered, imagining their digging up Rena's body. "And Rena wanted to tell those creatures how much God loved them!"

"She was always full of love," Betsy responded.

"And look at how she was repaid!"

When the grave was filled, Daniel, Luke, and Jeremy planted sagebrush over it and brushed sand around until the ground appeared as undisturbed as the surrounding desert.

Abby returned to camp, unable to endure another instant.

At last Zeke summoned the wagons into position for Benjamin Talbot again, then bellowed the familiar "Wagons, ho-o!"

Walking alongside the oxen, Abby stared out at the landscape. This entire desolate landscape along the Humboldt with its sagebrush, patchy grass, and dust was Rena's grave. This is what she would remember when she thought of Rena—a beautiful young woman who had been killed by this loathsome land and this senseless trek west. Abby wished that the blazing sun might obliterate her memory of this place.

That night Martha gave birth to a daughter and named her Rena. The tiny baby, however, possessed thick black hair and bore no resemblance to the Rena everyone had loved.

For days the wagons crossed the strange terrain, and the thought constantly crossed Abby's mind that death awaited all of them in unseen dangers at every bend of the trail. Sometimes the river snaked off into impassable canyons, and the trail swung over sage-covered bluffs for miles before they could return to their poor excuse of a river. High water forced them to take further detours. And often they had to cross the river to trek for a few miles, and then ford back again.

A week after Rena's funeral, Abby was washing clothes in the river water when Daniel appeared. She bristled at the sight of him, turning her back. *Stay away from me!* she thought. *I will not be hurt again!*

"It's dangerous for you to be alone here with the Diggers always about," he said.

"Jenny was washing clothes with me just minutes ago."

"She told me you wanted to be here alone," he replied. "You know it's not safe."

Abby shrugged with attempted nonchalance.

"I know that you must miss Rena," he said, "but something else must be wrong. What's happened to make you so unhappy, Abby?"

She no longer cared how beautiful her name sounded from his lips; she no longer cared about anything. "All of you who wanted to come on this trip are insane!" she flung at him.

"Perhaps you're right," he replied.

She wrung the alkaline water from her yellow calico dress and decided not to respond. Casting a sidelong glance, she saw that he had found a comfortable place to sit on the bank and watch her. If she did not have to finish her washing, she would depart with dispatch.

"It's this desert wilderness that makes everyone seem mad," he said, then gave a small smile. "Maybe it's not all bad either. Dryden said, 'Great wits are sure to madness near allied . . . and thin partitions do their bounds divide.'"

Abby retorted, "Great wits have nothing to do with it. I'm talking about out-and-out insanity."

Daniel did not reply.

"Surely with your vast store of quotations you must have something else to say."

He looked out across the river. "I was thinking that the difference between an insane man and a fool is said to be that the fool draws a wrong conclusion from a right principle, while an insane person draws a just inference from a false principle."

Perhaps that explained why Christians seemed so different, she mused. They drew their conclusions from a different set of principles.

The river meandered sluggishly past them, its stench putrid. Daniel spoke into the silence, "What are you thinking about so seriously?"

She scrubbed at the dirtied hem of her yellow calico dress. "Aunt Jessica told me when I first moved to Independence how delicate Rena's health was. It only seems inevitable that she would die on a trip like this."

"Rena came for a cause far greater than herself."

"For God?" Abby asked angrily.

"Yes, in most part for God."

You are insane, every one of you! she thought again, furiously wringing out the dress. She tossed it into the basket on top of the rest of her washing.

Daniel rose. "Here, let me help you."

Abby grabbed the basket and jerked it from him. "You are all mad!" she cried as she hurried away. "And I am equally so to have traveled with you!"

After that encounter, Daniel appeared to avoid Abby as determinedly as she attempted to avoid him. Yet when she remembered how rudely she had treated him, her eyes filled with tears of regret. Fortunately in the awful August heat, tears dried immediately. In any event, too many barriers stood between them now— Rena, Daniel's faith . . . Just recently Seth Thompson

192

had preached that Christians should not be yoked in marriage to unbelievers, and it seemed to Abby that he had been speaking to Daniel and her. Well, Seth Thompson could save his breath as far as she was concerned!

The Humboldt River's water deteriorated with every mile, becoming increasingly tepid and alkaline. The water's color changed from milky-white to yellowish-green as it seeped into marshes and finally into the evil-smelling sink. To Abby's mind, each of them had deteriorated just as badly, barely struggling along, hunger their constant companion.

After their two-day rest at the sink, they trekked through a dry stretch of fifteen miles to camp by a pond of brackish water. "This be the last grass 'n water 'til we pull through Forty-mile Desert," Zeke Wilkes warned.

They are all mad, Abby thought again, *and I am going mad too.* Not that madness here was unique. The captain of a wagon train they had passed told of several of his people who had gone insane. "An' if they ain't all crazy now, they will be in Forty-mile Desert!"

If the Humboldt Sink was terrible, the Forty-mile Desert was worse. Leveling out in all directions, encrusted with white alkaline, the earth was baked hard. Each step seared their feet, and every parched day stretched out to an unbearable eternity. A saliva pebble under Abby's tongue scarcely helped. When she attempted to look at the dazzling horizon, her eyes swam and dots danced across the burning landscape. No living thing showed itself, neither lizard nor Digger Indian.

Daniel appeared before her out of the burning sunset one evening with a diffident nod of greeting. "Abby, I'm afraid that Marigold and Daisy are too weakened—"

"Then shoot them!" she replied coldly.

He frowned. "I am going to have to."

"Then be done with it! It does not surprise me at all!" This time when the shots rang out, she scarcely flinched.

Walking alongside the oxen one scorching afternoon, her thoughts turned for relief to memories of New York and then to Miss Sheffield's School and to Rose. She envisioned again her own carefree existence until the evening Daniel and Uncle Benjamin had arrived and her fine life had been ruined. What was it that Rose had said that night in their room? "Place it in God's hands . . ."

Rose reminded her of Rena with her faith. What if *she* were certain of God? She peered out into the glaring light. "Where are You, God?" she cried out across the desert. "Where are You?"

Thad turned back from driving the oxen and shot a peculiar look at her, but she simply returned his stare. What did it matter what he and the others thought!

Not long afterward, Betsy joined her again, probably sent by Aunt Jessica. They walked along together, saying little, simply enduring.

One afternoon Betsy cried, "Look . . . a lake! Don't you see the blue and the trees?"

Abby said wearily, "Close your eyes and then open them again."

Betsy reluctantly obeyed. "It's gone . . ."

"Another mirage, like so much in life."

Abby noted the clouds of dejection on Betsy's face. She was no longer the bright, cheery girl who had met her with such enthusiasm that first night in Independence—and just as well. Now she would not become disappointed in what life offered.

When they reached the hot springs gushing into the air, Horace shouted, wild-eyed, "I'm turning back! No one will read my newspaper in such a god-forsaken place!"

"Educated people live in Yerba Buena," Daniel

assured him. "It is not like this at all. It's on the Bay of San Francisco, with cool ocean breezes."

"I don't believe you!" Horace replied as he stared at the boiling geysers. "No one told us how terrible this trip would be . . . about this desert . . . water boiling from the earth! Nobody warned us . . ."

"None of us have ever been in this desert before except Zeke," Daniel explained.

"I'm turning back . . . turning back!" Horace cried.

At last Benjamin Talbot convinced him to go on one more day, and continued to persuade him, day after day.

Abby carried Horace's supper to him one evening. His lantern jaw hung slack and his green eyes vacillated from vacant to wild. His breakdown was her fault in part, she told herself. He had been attracted to her, and she had rebuffed him. Love again; love brought nothing but woe. How much better to remain cold and sealed off, drawing deep into the recesses of one's self.

The next day they traveled in silence across a sandy ridge, the sand becoming deeper and deeper until Sarah's two lead oxen sank knee-deep. They struggled in the hot sand, bellowing hideously, their legs broken.

Zeke's rifle shots sounded again.

Sarah's wagon had sunk to the axle, which snapped. "It's past fixin'," Zeke decided, helping Sarah unload her belongings into Abby's wagon. Her two remaining oxen were joined with Abby's, and they left the wagon behind. As they moved on, Abby glanced back at it. The hulks of five dead oxen and Sarah's wagon lay half sunken in the desert graveyard.

"Don't matter anyhow," Sarah said, plodding along beside her.

Travel was easier on the sagebrush-covered downgrade, and finally Abby caught sight of cottonwoods along a river. *Another mirage,* she warned herself morosely, but it was real. The Truckee River . . . California! or at least nearby since no one knew precisely where the territory began.

Abby's spirits lifted, along with those of her traveling companions. When the oxen scented the river, there was no stopping them; they rushed for the water.

The emigrants rested and repaired the wagons all day Friday while the oxen grazed. That evening after their rabbit stew, Reverend Thompson announced, "We will be having our first wedding tomorrow evening. Sarah and Zeke will marry. They invite you to attend the ceremony."

Some of them raised a feeble but surprised cheer, and the women took stock of provisions they could pool for the wedding supper. There was no sugar. And only the Schmitts had flour, a small amount. "Might be deer hereabouts," one of the men said, and they formed a hunting party.

Abby pondered Sarah's decision. Why would she marry the old guide? The rest of them had become gaunt, but once-massive Sarah looked rather pretty now. Abby's curiosity must have been apparent for Sarah confided, "Ain't no good bein' alone at night, 'n Zeke wants to settle. He's got a ranch in California fer runnin' cattle."

The wedding ceremony took place alongside the swift Truckee River. Benjamin Talbot gave Sarah away again, and Betsy held the gold ring—the very wedding ring that Samuel had given to Sarah in January. Zeke had trimmed his gray beard and hair and brought out a cleaner buckskin outfit. Sarah wore her old white wedding dress, the seams taken in considerably; her sun-bleached hair was coiled in her usual bun at the nape of her neck. She looked so lovely that Zeke seemed dazzled. Standing at his side, Sarah repeated the vows. "I, Sarah, take thee, Ezekiel, to be my wedded . . ."

196

Abby felt Daniel's eyes upon her and ignored him. There was nothing for them now. Nothing.

She turned her attention to the Talbot family, all with clean hair and wearing clean clothing again. How they had changed since Sarah's first wedding. Aunt Jessica's gaunt face was deeply lined; Uncle Benjamin's hair, nearly white; Betsy had grown taller, thin, and serious; Jenny and Jeremy appeared saddened; Martha held her new baby while Luke held the hands of the twins, quieter now. The most dire change, of course, was Rena's absence.

Seth Thompson pronounced the familiar words: "Forasmuch as Ezekiel and Sarah have consented together in holy wedlock, and have witnessed the same before God and this company, and hereto have pledged their faith each to the other . . ."

After the final prayer, Zeke kissed his bride with unabashed pleasure. The hunters had brought down a deer, and for the wedding supper there was roasted venison, beans, wild greens, and ten small biscuits. Afterward they sang, and Andrew Jacqueman played his fiddle.

Sarah moved to Zeke's tent, and Abby thought again of the hired girl's words, "Ain't no good bein' alone nights." *What would it be like to be held in Daniel's arms?* she reflected for an instant, then turned the tortuous thought away.

CHAPTER 20

THEY TOILED INTO THE CALIFORNIA MOUNTAINS along the Truckee River for over a week. It was steady uphill work all the way, though there was water and grass again for the stock. The growth changed from sagebrush and scrubby pines to patches of forest as they crossed and recrossed the boulder-strewn river, shivering in the icy water, fighting its swift current. They climbed higher and higher into the mountains. At nine thousand feet, they labored for breath and tired quickly. The route was the most precipitous they had traveled, and the men and oxen strained in their efforts to lift the wagons up the nearly vertical mountain walls. High above them, snow-capped peaks rose, even now in early September.

Finally they eased the wagons down into Bear Valley by snubbing ropes around the trees. Progress was slow. Each day they met harrowing obstacles. The California Mountains were beautiful with their sheer passes and gleaming crags above, but Abby no longer cared for their beauty, nor anything else.

When the sun began to set at their camp in

Emigrant Gap, she sat on her wagon seat, lonely and exhausted. She had never in her life felt so wrenchingly alone. Life offered nothing. It seemed senseless to carry on at all. Beyond tears, her despair drew her down into darkness, a vast black wilderness that entangled her mind and her soul.

From the depths of despondency something within her recalled Rose's words: "Place it in God's hands . . ."

And then Rena—What was it that Rena had asked Seth to read from his Bible? She reached for Rena's Bible and reluctantly opened it to the ribbon marker. Yes, here it was, underlined. She read in the sunset. "There was a man of the Pharisees, named Nicodemus, a ruler of the Jews: The same came to Jesus by night, and said unto him, Rabbi, we know that thou art a teacher come from God: for no man can do these miracles that thou doest, except God be with him. Jesus answered and said unto him, Verily, verily, I say unto thee, Except a man be born again, he cannot see the kingdom of God."

Abby thumbed through the pages, reading Rena's underlined words. "For God so loved the world, that he gave his only begotten Son, that whosoever believeth in him should not perish, but have everlasting life."

The words seemed alive, and she read on, page after page, drawn along by she knew not what, only that it seemed possible she might discover wisdom in these pages . . . that she might even discover the purpose of her life. "Jesus saith unto him, I am the way, the truth, and the life; no man cometh unto the Father, but by me."

She was weary of resentments, despair, and fear. She had struggled and debated and doubted for so long now, and suddenly she simply wanted to see if God was real, if the gospel was true. *Now is the time,* a small still voice within her seemed to say. *Now is the time.*

199

She recalled Seth Thompson's preaching that the Holy Spirit would not strive forever with one to come to God.

No, the familiar voice of despair within her protested, *you must not give in to this.*

Now is the time—the softer, loving voice urged.

She remembered Daniel's words when she first heard of the family scandal. "You must forgive them . . . your father, your mother, the woman. You must forgive them."

And the loving voice within her echoed his words: *You must forgive them if you want to know God.*

The strident voice protested, *It's entirely irrational!*

She ignored it. "I want to forgive them," she whispered, then by an act of will added, "I *do* forgive them."

A tear slid down her cheek and her resistance began to crumble. Her lips trembled as she gazed out toward the sunset and said, "O Lord Jesus, I do repent of my sins—my pride, my dark wishes and jealousy about Rena. I want this new birth. I want to believe. I give my life to You . . . make of me what You will. Amen."

She caught a deep breath and let the air out slowly, then awaited an answer—a great voice from the clouds lying across the sunset . . . lightning striking a nearby pine tree . . .

For a long time she heard only the chirping of birds in the pines, then slowly, slowly she felt peace flow into her heart, peace as she had never known it, peace that passed understanding. As she stood there, the trees became greener and the mountains became beautiful beyond belief. The very air glistened, and she felt compelled to fall to her knees. Thanksgiving welled up within her and flowed from her heart. "Thank You! Oh, thank You!" she prayed, her arms upraised to Him as if in an ancient rite.

Sudden joy burst through her like a golden radiance, and she glowed with His love, feeling at one with the glorious sunset, at one with the universe. She wished that she might go on with Him like this forever, that her spirit might always be with Him. She realized that this was the fulfillment for which she had always yearned—knowing Him. The emptiness within her was at last overflowing with joy. She was scarcely aware that darkness fell, and that night in her wagon she was so pervaded with His love that she fell asleep murmuring her Savior's wondrous name.

The next morning she awakened with the first light of dawn. Peering out the puckering-string hole at the back of the wagon, she marveled at the mountains and the sky's magnificence. She felt wonderfully refreshed and overflowing with joy. It was Sunday and, though she had always appreciated the day for its rest, she had never looked forward this eagerly to their morning services. Now expectation beamed around her like the sun's morning rays. Rough travel and the unknown still lay ahead, but now the prospect—the entire prospect of life—promised excitement and adventure.

She slipped into her favorite blue calico dress and swept back her hair into a chignon. Peering into her small mirror, she saw that her eyes were no longer dull, but lively with anticipation.

She stepped out of the wagon. The mountainsides of Emigrant Gap surrounded her, lush and green with tall ponderosa and juniper and sugar pine, their fragrance filling the air. Around them were great boulders, some bigger than the mansion on Union Square. She hurried to the stream and washed her face in the cool, clear water, then set out to climb a boulder for the sheer pleasure of it.

Later, as she helped Sarah get breakfast, Betsy asked, "What's happened to you?"

Abby's joy bubbled out in laughter. "Something

wonderful!'' She realized Daniel had taken note of it too, and she smiled at the confusion on his face.

After breakfast she returned to her wagon and recalled Rena's final request that Abby read the last few pages of her diary. How could she have forgotten? How? She opened Rena's trunk and found the diary on top of her cousin's belongings.

Thumbing through the bound book, she saw that Rena had written a letter to her on its last pages. To think that she had been foremost in Rena's thoughts just before her death . . . to think that Rena had cared for her this much! Tears of gratitude stung her eyes and she had to calm herself to read.

> *Along the Humboldt River*

> *Dearest Abby,*
>
> *I love you so very much, and I know that your feelings about me must be very confused for I realize that you are deeply in love with Daniel. As you have probably guessed, everyone has always thought that he and I would someday marry. The peculiar thing is that I have always known that I would never marry at all. Daniel never proposed or even hinted about marriage. We love each other dearly, but it is simply a great Christian love between a man and woman who love the Lord.*
>
> *I shall try to explain. When I was a sickly and difficult child, it was Daniel who told me about Christ's dying on the cross for our sins so that He might lead us back to our heavenly Father. Although my parents were devout believers, it was Daniel who had to show me the way, the truth, and the life eternal. This is our great bond.*
>
> *I know that Daniel loves you, but he knows—as Seth preached last Sunday—that believers should not be yoked to unbelievers. And so I pray for your salvation every day. When you have found the Lord—for I know in my spirit that you will—you must never allow my memory to stand between the two of you.*
>
> *In this past year, I have felt that I would not live much longer. Now it appears that I will not finish this journey, though I did so want to help carry God's love westward.*

202

Do not grieve for me, my dear cousin, for I rejoice at being with the Lord in glory.

> With His love,
> Rena

Abby reread the letter, tears streaming down her cheeks. Rena had indeed carried God's love westward to the very last moment. In retrospect, it was Rena's final request for Seth to read about being born again that especially touched Abby's heart now for she knew Rena had done it for her.

O Lord, Abby prayed, *help me to carry Thy banner in Rena's place. Help me to carry it to the very last instant of my life on earth!*

As for Daniel, having him love her no longer seemed of such overwhelming importance. *I place that in Thy hands, Lord,* she prayed. *I place that in Thy hands.*

On the way to the wooded site Seth had chosen for their Sunday morning service, Abby gathered up wildflowers. She arrived long before the others and arranged the flowers reverently at the base of the cross, praising God for His love. The fragrance of pines drifted on the soft morning breeze, and birds sang from all around the wooded glen. After a while she became aware of someone's presence, and she knew in her spirit who it was. She turned. Yes . . . Daniel.

He beamed, approaching her with wonder. "You have found Him . . . you've found the Lord, haven't you?"

"Yes. How did you know?"

"I saw the joy and love all around you this morning . . . and when I arrived here to pray just minutes ago, there you were on your knees arranging flowers by the cross."

As she looked at Daniel, at this good godly man, it

seemed that God was smiling upon them in the shafts of sunshine streaming through the pine trees.

"I've prayed for you every day, sometimes every hour," Daniel said. "I've never prayed so much for anyone . . . since that moment I met you in Miss Sheffield's sitting room and saw your life breaking up before you. I know now that I already loved you—" He faltered, coloring from the edges of his beard to his forehead.

"You loved me then?"

He nodded. "When I saw you coming down the stairway of Miss Sheffield's, it seemed that God was saying, 'This is the one, this is the one I have chosen for you!'"

"Oh, Daniel, you told me that I must never say this to a man, but I love you too! I love you!"

He caught her in his arms and for a long moment they simply gazed at each other. "God is so good, so wonderful, His timing so perfect," Daniel exulted. "I couldn't be patient much longer! Will you marry me now, Abby . . . now . . . today . . . as soon as possible? I don't have a ring yet, but I do have a special gift for you." He took a soft leather pouch from his shirt pocket. From the pouch, he withdrew something wrapped in white silk.

As he removed the silk, Abby could scarcely believe her eyes. Her grandmother's sapphire pendant glowed in the morning sunlight.

He said simply, "I always knew someday I'd return it to you."

"*You* purchased it, Daniel. You saved it for me."

"Yes." He smiled ironically. "And now I'm trying to tempt you into marrying me for it."

"Oh, Daniel! Oh, yes! But I would have accepted without anything."

He drew her into his arms again, and their lips met with sweet yearning and tenderness. In the fragrance of pines and the choir of bird song, it felt as though

God had filled and surrounded them with His joy and love.

Benjamin Talbot announced the news after the morning worship service. "We have a special celebration tonight, a fitting conclusion to this last part of our trek. It gives me great pleasure to invite all of you to a wedding." He beamed. "It's Abby and Daniel!"

The Talbots cheered and hugged the two of them— the women "having guessed it all along" and the men stunned.

The emigrants threw themselves into wedding preparations with joyous abandon. Even Horace Litmer managed to congratulate her and Daniel.

Later, Abby stood in Sarah's white wedding gown while Aunt Jessica delightedly pinned in the seams. Abby confided, "I can scarcely believe this is happening to me. It seems as unlikely as our being only a week's travel from Sutter's Fort."

"I don't think any of us can believe that yet!" her aunt agreed. "Only one week and all downhill."

After a moment Abby said, "I'm grateful that Horace's enthusiasm for printing a newspaper is returning."

Her aunt nodded as she fitted a side seam. Removing the pin from between her lips she said, "I've prayed for him for a long time."

"You must have been praying for me too," Abby said. "You and Daniel and Rena and . . . who knows who else!"

"Only the entire family!"

Tremulous, Abby turned for her aunt to pin the other side seam. "I can never thank you enough."

"But you can. You can thank us by praying for others all of your life."

"I will. I promise I will."

Aunt Jessica added, "And you and the other girls could keep my roses and lilacs blooming wherever you go."

"We will! Oh, we surely will! And they'll always be known as Aunt Jessica's roses and Aunt Jessica's lilacs." Ignoring the pins in the wedding dress, she caught her aunt in a hug. "I promise for all of us."

When they returned to the fitting Abby said, "I'm going to miss everyone from the train." Sarah and Zeke would head south to his ranch; the Jacquemans, to the coast to plant vineyards; the Schmitts, north to farming land. The rest of them would settle near Sutter's Fort.

"We'll all miss each other after enduring this trek together." Aunt Jessica suddenly smiled. "But let's set our minds on this wonderful wedding. Daniel told Benjamin that he doesn't have a ring, and I thought that you might like to borrow mine until he can buy one. I'm finally thin enough to be able to take it off again, and it would give me such pleasure to see Daniel place it on your finger." She removed the gold ring and proffered it.

"But don't you think lending it will bring bad luck?"

Aunt Jessica laughed. "I don't believe in luck, Abby. I believe in the Lord. Here, my dear, why don't you try it on?"

That evening Abby stood with Benjamin Talbot on the edge of the piney glade, listening to Andre Jacqueman play the wedding prelude on his fiddle. She wore the refitted white gown, a splash of *Fleur-de-lis* in remembrance of Rose, and Grandmother Talbot's beautiful sapphire pendant. Her hand went to the pendant, and her heart filled with happiness again at Daniel's keeping it all of this time for her.

Uncle Benjamin whispered just above the music, "You do look like your Grandmother Talbot."

Abby remembered the lovely woman in the portrait, her eyes aglow with faith. "Do you think she knows I have accepted the Lord as my Savior?"

"The Bible says, 'there is joy in the presence of the angels of God over one sinner that repenteth.' I wouldn't be surprised if angels tell our loved ones."

The prelude came to its concluding notes, and her uncle gallantly offered his arm to escort her into the glade, "Ready now, Abby?"

"Oh, yes!" Her bouquet of wildflowers trembled slightly when the company began to sing the song she had requested, the words filling the air in the first rays of the sunset:

> Amazing grace! how sweet the sound,
> That saved a wretch like me!
> I once was lost, but now am found,
> Was blind, but now I see.

As she and Uncle Benjamin made their way through the emigrants, she stored the beauty of the scene in her memory so that she might paint it someday— *Marrying Daniel*.

Standing at the front of the glade, he wore the handsome black suit she had first seen him wearing that evening at Miss Sheffield's door; now he proudly awaited her beside the cross. His blue eyes held hers as they both sang with the others:

> 'Twas grace that taught my heart to fear,
> And grace my fears relieved;
> How precious did that grace appear
> The hour I first believed!

Tears welled in Abby's eyes as she remembered Rena's melodious contralto rising through the others during the fourth verse, and it seemed that somehow she was among them again, singing:

> When we've been there ten thousand years,
> Bright shining as the sun,
> We've no less days to sing God's praise
> Than when we first begun.

Seth Thompson began the service. "Dearly beloved, we are gathered together here in the sight of God and in the presence of these witnesses to join together this man and this woman in holy matrimony, which is an honorable estate, signifying unto us the mystical union which exists between Christ and His church—"

Abby and Daniel listened to the words as one. ". . . the union of husband and wife in heart, body, and mind . . ."

Then Seth was saying to Uncle Benjamin, "Who giveth this woman to be married to this man?"

Benjamin Talbot replied with love, "I do."

Daniel repeated the familiar vows, his eyes overflowing with love. "I, Daniel, take thee, Abigail, to be my wedded wife, to have and to hold, from this day forward, for better, for worse, for richer, for poorer, in sickness and in health, to love and to cherish, as long as we both shall live."

And then she spoke, "I, Abigail, take thee, Daniel, to be my wedded husband, to have and to hold from this day forward . . ."

It seemed only moments before Daniel placed Aunt Jessica's gold wedding ring on Abby's finger.

"Those whom God hath joined together, let not man put asunder," Seth pronounced. He blessed them and looked at Daniel. "You may now kiss the bride."

Betsy beamed as she accepted the bouquet of wildflowers, and Abby turned to Daniel.

His strong arms encircled her, and his lips touched hers softly for an instant, then with such mounting and joyous passion that it did seem they were stealing fire from heaven. Surrounded and filled with love, they scarcely heard the emigrants' cheer.

ABOUT THE AUTHOR

ELAINE SCHULTE is a wife, mother of two sons, and a writer whose short stories, articles, and novels have been published around the world. Her first inspirational novel for Zondervan was ON WINGS OF LOVE, a contemporary story; two additional contemporaries, SONG OF JOY and ECHOES OF LOVE, are forthcoming. WESTWARD, MY LOVE is her first historical novel. Its sequel, the story of Abby's roommate, Rose, and her precarious trip to California by clipper ship, is DREAMS OF GOLD.